Canadian **Dani Collins** knew in high school that she wanted to write romance for a living. Twenty-five years later, after marrying her high school sweetheart, having two kids with him, working at several generic office jobs and submitting countless manuscripts, she got The Call. Her first Mills & Boon novel won the Reviewers' Choice Award for Best First in Series from *RT Book Reviews*. She now works in her own office, writing romance.

To my son, Sam, who made the mistake of calling me
when I was stuck after bringing Rozalia and Viktor to
the chalet in the Carpathians. Sam suggested they go
dancing in the village square, with lights strung above
the dance floor and arches of flowers, like at a wedding.
I had to cut the scene in later drafts, but the image
got me writing. So, thank you, Sam. I only wish I could
offer such elegant coding solutions should you
ever be stuck while programming. xo

CHAPTER ONE

"No entry, miss."

The middle-aged man in a uniform spoke in heavily accented English. He wore an air of boredom, not even looking at Rozalia Toth as he turned her away from the gate of Kastély Karolyi.

"The best photos are from up the hill." He pointed.

She couldn't blame him for thinking she was one more tourist milling on the sidewalk, eager for shots of the gorgeous architecture here in Budapest. On her way to the gate, she had snapped the front of the Rohan family home, thinking to show it to her family when she got back to New York.

It was so beautiful, who could resist? Intricate gray brickwork was covered in centuries of vines and framed by lush old maples and oaks. The scrupulously manicured flower beds splashed color around the wide staircase that formed the covered entryway. Tall windows were spaced evenly across both floors with wrought iron balconies jutting out from a few at the top. Adorable round gables and a chimney on top made it storybook perfect.

She would have been charmed even without the familial connection—of which hers was virtually nonexistent. Even so, she intended to exploit it.

"I have an appointment with Mara Rohan," she said in Hungarian.

"Name?"

"Rozalia Toth. She's expecting my cousin, Gisella Drummond. I've come in her place." She had thought about emailing ahead to warn about the change of plan, but had gambled they would be less likely to turn her away if she was here in person.

She gazed on the house again, listening to the guard radio her name, sorry that Gisella couldn't be here with her. Through childhood and years of schooling, as they both gained their degrees and apprenticed as goldsmiths, they had longed to see their family's "old country."

Rozalia, in particular, had always been curious about the family history. But rather than walk the narrowest alleys of Budapest to find the walk-up where their grandmother had been born, or drive into the countryside to locate her own grandfather's birthplace, she had been drawn here to Kastély Karolyi.

Istvan Karolyi would have been her grandfather if he hadn't died in the revolution. Instead, he was only Gisella's grandfather. Their grandmother, Eszti, had met him while they were attending university. When she became pregnant, Istvan asked her to marry him, offering a pair of family earrings in lieu of an engagement ring. He then sent her to America ahead of him, to escape the unrest. He died before he could join her and Eszti later married Rozalia's grandfather, but still held a small torch for her first love.

That sort of titanic romance went straight to Rozalia's soft heart. She needed to know *everything* about it.

And, like Gisella, she yearned to get her hands on those earrings, separated just as Eszti and Istvan had been. Rozalia and her cousin had searched for years for them, wanting to give them back to their grandmother so she could hold again that token from her first love.

A message came back to the guard that Mara Rohan had left town. The guard asked if someone else would take the meeting.

Rozalia perked up in anticipation that Mara's son, Viktor, would admit her. He was *gorgeous*. And a count, not that Hungary allowed their nobility to use their titles, but it was one more thing that made him ultraintriguing.

From the moment Rozalia had searched his name, she'd been enthralled with the look of him—all dark and brooding with short black hair, a strong brow line and a squared-off, clean-shaven jaw. His mouth was the most intriguing. His upper lip was narrow, but formed with two well-defined peaks. The bottom was full and bitable—not that she had ever let herself go enough to nibble on a man's bottom lip, but he certainly put the idea into her head.

One near-naked shot of him on the beach had jump-started a million fantasies. She was only human, for heaven's sake. He'd been caught as he emerged with snorkel and fins in his hands, the most impossibly small bathing suit straining to cover his naughty bits. The rest of him was pure muscle, abs flat, dark nipples sharpened by the chill against the swarthy plane of his chest. His expression as he realized he was being photographed was positively filthy, he was so disgusted at whoever had taken the shot.

Why that made her laugh, she didn't know, but she had been drawn here as much by the opportunity to meet that man as she was by the chance to acquire her grandmother's earring.

The security guard received a response and shook his head, repeating in English the message she had understood in Hungarian as clearly as he had.

"Your appointment is canceled."

So much for showing up in person making it harder to turn her away. Rozalia set her back teeth and found a pleasant smile. "May I reschedule?"

"No." He didn't bother checking with the voice on the radio for that one.

"May I leave a note?"

His cheek ticked, but he let her stand there and scribble in her notebook. She said she was sorry to have missed the chance to speak with the family and that she would be in the city for several more days, then added the name of her hotel and her contact details.

She tore out the sheet and handed it to the guard. He would no doubt crumple it, but she thanked him and started back to her hotel.

She waited until she was out of his earshot before releasing her disparaging snort.

She had spent the best part of a decade tracking her grandmother's earrings. She wasn't about to give up *that* easily.

Viktor Rohan was mentally sorting a dozen priorities as he left Rika Corp and descended the stairs toward his waiting car.

A young woman, a backpacker, if the map she held was anything to go by, stood chatting up his driver. The spring breeze pressed the fabric of her T-shirt against her modest chest and lifted the waves of her loose brunette hair away from her creamy complexion. She wore no makeup, but sunshine was all she needed. That buttermilk skin would light up any room—most specifically a darkened bedroom.

Viktor didn't begrudge his driver a personal life, but for some reason, as his employee leaned in to make a play for this one, Viktor bristled. A compulsive *This one's for me* resounded in him.

He had grown out of picking up women, especially young, free-spirited ones, back when he'd still been nursing scorn over an adolescent heartbreak. From his midtwenties on, he'd preferred the convenience of longer-term arrangements with women in his social circle. Now that he was hitting thirty, however, even those comfortable situations came with expectations of a more serious future. His own mother badgered him ceaselessly to marry and produce an heir.

Perhaps his interest in this pretty traveler was reflexive pushback against his mother's latest efforts because he found himself mentally rearranging his priorities *again*, now allowing for a shared dinner this evening—with plenty of time allotted for other potential entertainments to develop.

"Joszef."

His driver snapped to attention and hurried to open the back door of his town car.

The woman turned to look at him and stilled as though transfixed. A slow smile filled her expression with even more light. He thought of artwork that depicted angels of grace and goddesses of fertility, none of which had ever caused such a brilliant thrust of heat to swell in him.

Oh, yes, this one was definitely his.

"That saves me going inside to ask for you." She came toward him, hand extended. "I'm pleased to meet you, Úr. Rohan."

She spoke in Hungarian without accent, but something told him she was American. He took her hand the way a cat snared a bird that flittered too close, pulling her in, determined she wouldn't get away.

Then she spoke again, and the hunter inside him went from playful to bloodthirsty, claws extending.

"I'm Rozalia Toth. Do you have time to speak with me?"

* * *

Viktor Rohan dropped her hand like she was made of fire. It was a shock when she was still reeling from that initial touch that had set her alight. The spark of generic attraction she'd experienced for an online image flared to sharp fascination as she faced him in person. A compulsion to know everything about this man welled in her.

"No," he answered with the look she had seen in that beach photograph, like he thought she was something irritating. Abhorrent, even. Definitely far beneath him. "How do you have the nerve to chase me down like this?"

He was so much more dynamic and dangerous in real life. An air of potent virility came off him along with ruthless command of his surroundings. It took everything in her to keep her faculties and respond, "I had an appointment with your mother. She promised to show me an antique earring that my grandmother possessed at one time, but she canceled at the last minute."

"You aren't the one who made the appointment and I advised her against agreeing to it, not when you haven't even offered an apology." He turned to step into the space of the open car door.

"You're right. I'm sorry. I should have been clear that I took Gisella's place."

He swiveled a look on her that should have sent her head rolling into the street. "I meant an apology from your grandmother. For stealing our family heirloom."

"What? Grandmamma didn't *steal* those earrings. Why on earth do you think that?"

He narrowed his eyes. "I don't think it. I know it." So confident, as if it was a proven fact. He folded himself into the back of his car.

"Wait! That's wrong." She pushed herself into the space behind the door, so his driver couldn't slam it without breaking her shins. She braced a hand on the top of the door as she leaned her head down. "Your great-uncle gave them to her as an engagement present."

"How is that possible? He was dead before they went missing. Joszef," he said sharply.

The driver, who'd been doing his best to charm the socks—and everything else—off her a minute ago, set his hand on her arm.

Rozalia had long ago learned how to shake off a grope in the subway and cast a warning look that had any man stepping back in defense of his chestnuts. The driver did exactly that, one hand blocking his fly on reflex.

She also knew better than to get into cars with strangers, but that's exactly what she did. She pushed into the back seat, trying to crawl across him like she was taking the far chair in a row at the theater.

It was rude enough, and startled Viktor so that he grabbed her waist to steady her in front of him, practically on his lap. His strength was undeniable, but what froze her in place was the impact of his touch. For a moment, they were eye to eye, nose tip to nose tip, practically about to kiss.

His eyes were gray as an ashen sky, moody and ominous without any hint of blue. And dear *Lord* he had an erotic mouth.

Her hand was on the leather seat next to his thigh, but she longed to brace against the well-developed ball of his shoulder. Touch the heat of his neck. He smelled of something woodsy and spicy, fine wool and the barest hint of brandy.

All of that combined with the flash in his stormy gaze to give her the vertigo she experienced looking down from tall buildings. The flip-flop in her stomach warned of a life-threatening fall even though she knew she was perfectly safe.

"Sir?" Joszef said.

With a muscular twist, Viktor dumped Rozalia onto the seat beside him.

"Close the door," he said.

It slammed.

He settled his arm along the back of the seat so he was angled toward her, silently asking, *What now?*

Because she was trapped. The luxury sedan had a roomy interior, but it became unbearably small and airless. She felt enclosed with a panther. A hungry one. Her feet were still tangled with his and she carefully withdrew them to her side of the car.

"Are you finished work for the day? Can I buy you a drink?" she asked. Somewhere reputable and crowded, preferably. "I'd like to talk this out. I always understood that Istvan died *after* he gave Grandmamma the earrings."

She was using her conciliatory *I* statements deliberately. The family didn't call her their number one mediator for nothing.

"You're wrong." No compromise in his tone. "She came to the house after he was killed, stole my great-grandmother's earrings, sold one to escape to America and sold the other one when she arrived."

Now she was growing annoyed.

"My grandmother is a very kind and honest person. She would never steal and certainly wouldn't lie, especially to family. I don't know how the story got so twisted. How did you even wind up with one earring? How long have you had it?"

"My grandmother Dorika dealt in art during Soviet times. She came across it and knew how rare and valuable it was, despite it only being one of a pair."

Rozalia frowned. "Didn't she recognize it as her mother's?"

"She was on my father's side. My mother is the Karolyi descendant. And yes, Dorika knew immediately it was Cili Karolyi's. Anyone else would have broken the setting to sell the stones, but she tucked it away as a bargaining chip."

If she wore pearls, Rozi would have clutched them, she was so appalled by the thought of the setting being broken. But, "What kind of 'bargaining chip'?"

"Enticement when she arranged my parents' marriage. She knew my mother would want it. Those earrings should have passed down through the women in our family."

He was trying to make her feel guilty about her grandmother's supposed theft, but she was caught by the rest of what he'd said.

"She arranged your parents' marriage? I didn't know that was a thing that was done here."

"This level of success isn't accidental," Viktor said dryly, flicking a hand to indicate the car's leather seats and privacy window, its polished wood grain trim and the touch screen computer mounted for his convenience. "It comes from generations of strategic alliances. *Not* from handing off priceless family jewels with a marriage promise to dishonest peasant girls."

Rozalia let her jaw hang open so he could appreciate the full extent of her affront. "Easy to see why your mother had to be bribed into marrying *that* sort of charm."

Dang. She hadn't meant to reveal the temper that got the better of her sometimes. She looked like a pushover, but she wasn't.

Nevertheless, the way his cheeks hollowed with thinning patience and his gaze frosted over gave her pause.

"What did you hope to accomplish by coming here, Ms. Toth? You're wasting my valuable time."

She scraped together her own patience, trying to salvage this trip. "I want to make you an offer for the earring."

"No." Flat and unequivocal.

"At least let me see it!"

"No."

"*Why not?* Even if Grandmamma had stolen it, *which she didn't*, what's the use in punishing *me* for that?"

"Why do you want to see it?"

"To take photos." She searched for her most reasonable, professional tone. "I'd like to appraise it properly."

His brows went up.

"I'm a fully qualified gemologist and goldsmith." She had apprenticed with her uncle Ben at Barsi on Fifth, the shop her grandfather had started after arriving in America. "I make custom pieces all the time. I'd like to take the measurements of the stones and grade them, make some sketches. If I can't purchase the original, I'd like to re-create the earrings for my grandmother. She's quite elderly." She also had health problems that had given them all a scare this winter, making it that much more imperative Rozalia succeed in her mission. "If I could give her that much, it would make her very happy."

"Aside from the fact I have no investment in your grandmother's happiness, am I to understand you want to make a copy? My mother has considered that several times, but the one-of-a-kind rarity is part of the earring's value. She'd rather have the authentic match and own the only pair. I'm in the process of acquiring the other one."

"Are you?" she asked with enough skepticism to turn his expression even stonier.

"You don't have the other one," he said with confidence.

She effected a casual shrug. "Not yet, but my cousin is in San Francisco right now." Probably getting shot down by a man Gisella considered to be her mortal enemy, but

Viktor didn't know that. Rozalia held Viktor's gaze while the pressure of his simmering anger nearly compressed her blood to a solid inside her veins.

"I suggest you advise him against getting in my way." His gaze slid to the fabric bag she had been carting around on her shoulder and held slouched in her lap.

"Her," Rozalia corrected with a blithe smile, not bothering to dig out her phone. She couldn't move. He would see she was trembling at the intensity of this confrontation. "The women in our family are very persuasive."

"I'll bet."

Hey.

"We're also very stubborn." She showed him the point of her chin. "I could call her, but Gisella is as determined as I am. Probably as determined as you are, seeing as she's Istvan's descendant and carries Karolyi blood. I'd say that gives her as much right to the earrings as you have." She blinked with innocence.

"Is she as foolhardy as you? Throwing herself in the way of a man with my resources?"

Rozalia refused to betray the seesaw of fear and exhilaration sending shivers through her whole body.

"If the earring is your mother's, she ought to be the one who decides whether to sell it to me. I only came here because she canceled our appointment. Why don't you call her and reschedule our meeting? Us womenfolk can work it out amongst ourselves." *Yes*, she assured him with a smile, she was patronizing him.

"My mother had to run to Visegrád. She won't be back for a week, at least."

"To see your great-aunt Bella? Istvan's sister?" Istvan had had two sisters, Bella and Viktor's grandmother Irenke, who had had Viktor's mother, Mara, and passed away some years ago. Rozalia had planned to track down

Bella if she had time, thinking she might be interested to know her brother's daughter and granddaughter lived in New York but—

"Do *not* interfere in my family, Ms. Toth. I will make your life very uncomfortable. In fact—" He pulled out his own phone and tapped to signal voice activation. "Text Kaine Michaels," he ordered, then dictated, "If you sell that earring to anyone but me, I will become a bigger problem than any you already have."

He hit the screen and a *whoosh* sounded.

Rozalia internally winced at the complication she'd just caused her cousin. *Sorry, Gizi.*

"Look, I didn't come here for a war." Time to try placating again. "Is it so unreasonable that I'm curious? Your mother was willing to talk to me. Why won't you let me buy you a drink and ask a few questions?"

"Because I don't like liars, Ms. Toth."

"When have I lied to you? I'm exactly what I appear to be. A long-lost relative—"

"You're not my relative," he stated with enough force it pushed her back an inch.

On the surface, it sounded like a rejection. Part of her was even a little stung by his vehemence. He didn't *want* to be associated with her, which was very insulting. Her brain was already gathering to make a haughty reply.

But as she met his gaze, a current of electricity crackled between them. His words took on new meaning. Even a necessary truth.

Her grandmother had been pregnant with Istvan Karolyi's daughter, Gisella's mother, when she came to America. Rozalia's mother was the product of Eszti's marriage to Benedek. All Rozalia's fascination with the Karolyi connection was wrapped up in the romance of the story. She didn't have a drop of blood tie in it.

Which made fantasizing about this man's bottom lip okay. Or rather, it was still a dumb thing to do, but at least it wasn't morally *wrong*.

Staring at it, she found herself longing to soothe the tension from the wide shape of it, lick and discover his taste and textures, feel his mouth cover hers and—

A strange light grew to a hot gleam in his gaze.

She realized she was *leaning in*.

With a small gasp, she pulled back, but he stayed exactly where he was, moving nothing but his eyes. He took his time sliding his perusal down her clean if wrinkled T-shirt and clean, faded jeans. Her chest grew tight, nipples stinging. Heat burned into her loins. Finally his gaze came back to what had to be a culpable expression on her face.

"Where are you staying?" His tone had gone from sandpaper to whiskey.

She swallowed. Licked her lips, drawing his gaze to her own mouth. Oh, dear.

"Um." For a second, she honestly couldn't recall. Then managed to give him the name of her hotel.

He dismissed it with a curl of his lip. "My place, then. We'll have dinner. You can show me exactly how persuasive you claim to be."

CHAPTER TWO

VIKTOR WATCHED THE pert Ms. Toth sit straight, looking wary and disconcerted when a moment ago she had been looking very...*receptive*. Her delicate scent had closed around him as they'd sat here, beguiling with its notes of vanilla and fresh air, sunscreen and something sensual and light and a tone he instinctively identified as *her*.

"You'll show me the earring?" she asked, eyeing him while showing him her profile.

"I'll give you an opportunity to tell me why I should."

A pause, then a small, decisive nod. "Fair enough."

He knocked on his window and told his driver where they were going. Then he wondered what the hell he was doing. Picking up a student taking a gap year would be bad enough. This woman was dangerous.

Not that she looked it. She projected innocence with her casual clothes and naked face. She chewed the corner of her mouth as though having second thoughts.

The virgin act wasn't normally his thing, but there was something in the way she nervously licked her lips that made desire dig sharp talons into his vitals. It wasn't a hunter's instinct to plunder the helpless. That wasn't his thing, either. Rather, he sensed she was quietly fighting a betrayal of her attraction toward him—one that exactly matched the sexual heat he was struggling against.

That was compelling.

In those seconds when she had looked at his mouth, silently begging him to ravage hers, he'd nearly given in to… Hell, had he ever felt such anticipation for a woman? His emotions had been buried alongside his brother, never to be resurrected. But as the hunger in her gaze had fixated on his lips, he'd felt something other than cynicism and the relentless press of obligation.

He had seen, oddly, an open door to freedom, when every other woman struck him as the bait inside a cage.

This one had to be bait, as well. She came from duplicitous stock, he reminded himself, redonning his cloak of skepticism. He didn't doubt she was the granddaughter of the woman who had stolen his great-grandmother's earrings, given the way she had misrepresented herself to steal into today's appointment. This doe-eyed innocence had to be an act to throw him off whatever it was that she really wanted.

It was very likely the way her grandmother had gotten the better of his great-uncle. Family legend had it that Istvan's thieving lover had claimed to be carrying a Karolyi bastard to gain entry to the house. The only reason his mother had agreed to meet Gisella was to ensure there wouldn't be any scandalous—and *false*—claims against the estate. There was such a thing as DNA testing and his mother had intended to insist on it.

Was that why Rozalia had come instead of the woman who would have had to undergo a blood test? He wondered what she *really* wanted. It couldn't be merely a glimpse of an earring. He would spare his mother the work of getting that answer by taking Rozalia Toth to Kastély Karolyi himself.

When they arrived, he had his driver pause to tell the gatekeeper to get rid of the paparazzi at the fence. As they carried on up the drive, beneath the bower of branches, he caught Rozalia sending him a pithy look.

He lifted a brow in query.

"They're just tourists, aren't they?" she said. "The house is listed in a guidebook as one of the best-preserved examples of classic architecture in Eastern Europe. I took a photo myself when I was here earlier today."

Something in that remark jarred, but he was also reminded of why he was of such interest to long-lens photographers right now. Damn his mother and her matchmaking and rumormongering. In her quest to see the next heir produced, she had singled out the daughter of a family friend—one of many associations cultivated over the last twenty years with the sole purpose that his mother would have the pick of the litter when the time came.

Trudi, an heiress from Austria, was suitably finished at boarding school. She excelled as a socialite, walking the line of interesting without being scandalous. She wrote freelance fashion articles and managed charity events for her father's auto manufacturing corporation—one that dovetailed nicely with some of Rika's steel interests. Viktor had had dinner with her twice. Both evenings were pleasantly civil and ended in an underwhelming kiss.

Yet his mother insisted on sowing whispers of a forthcoming announcement, trying to nudge him along. Trudi had signaled her interest by subletting a penthouse here in Budapest while she "helped" her friend curate a fashion line due out this fall. Mostly that involved making appearances in high-profile clubs and other trendy nightspots, amplifying her name so as to create the biggest splash in the headlines when the time came to announce their engagement.

Thus, the jackals were closing in, hoping for the scoop

of the year. It increased his trapped, prickly mood, feeding his compulsion to break free of expectations.

"Wow!" Rozalia said as they left the car and walked up the steps into the receiving hall. She flashed him an excited grin that invited him to cast off his brooding tension and join her in her enthusiasm. "It's like walking into a museum."

He rarely noticed the grandeur, but now took in the inlaid marble floors that were the craftsmanship of a nineteenth-century Italian master. Ornate mahogany trim and enormous gold-framed mirrors lined the walls. Chandeliers hung from a ceiling with murals and intricate plasterwork.

"Clearly built for impressing visitors," she murmured, lifting her gaze to the massive staircase. "I can picture all the ball gowns and powdered wigs. My cousin goes to the Met for their big events, but weddings are the only thing I've attended that are at all extravagant. Can you imagine what it must have been like?" She laughed at herself. "Maybe you know exactly what it's like. Do you have many balls?"

They were speaking English and he heard the *double entendre*.

"The usual amount," he replied dryly.

After the briefest confounded pause, she burst out laughing. It was, quite simply, the most beautiful laugh he had ever heard. He couldn't recall the last time he'd heard anyone laugh in this mausoleum. Not since he was a child. Her laughter echoed to the second-floor ceiling, seeming to catch in the chandelier and make it shiver with musical delight.

He was so caught by the sound, by the light and liveliness in her face, he felt his chest tingle with an urge to chuckle—which definitely hadn't happened since he was a child.

His butler, Endre, arrived to sober them. Endre offered to take the sorry-looking bag weighing her shoulder.

"To where?" she asked with a blink of surprise, then decided with a flashing smile, "I'll keep it." She set the worse-for-wear eyesore on the sofa as they entered the parlor, making Endre look like a dog whose tail had been stepped on.

They ordered drinks. Rozalia asked for *pálinka*, the Hungarian fruit brandy.

"When in Rome?" Viktor presumed.

"We drink it at family dinners. I could use the grounding influence right now. I'm having a hard time viewing this as your home. I wish Gisella was here to see it."

Rozalia was feeling like such a fraud. Like the poor cousin she had always been, standing in glamorous Gisella's shadow. Of *course* this was her cousin's heritage. She loved Gisella to pieces. In some ways Rozalia was closer to her than she was with her actual sister. She and Gizi were the same age and shared the same passion for metallurgy and gemology. Also for the lore of Grandmamma's earring and the determination to reunite the pieces and gift them to the woman they adored.

But Gisella was a willowy, stunning, spoiled only child. She wouldn't goggle in a place like this. She would assume she belonged here—which to some extent she did.

Rozalia, not so much.

She turned from glancing out the windows that faced the front gardens and saw that Viktor was watching her the way a cat watches a mouse when it is too lazy to leap just yet. Biding his time.

She searched for a resemblance to her beloved cousin, hoping the familiarity would reassure her, but only found a superficial similarity in coloring and height. He was a lot colder and more imposing than anyone she had ever encountered in her life.

Gisella would know how to handle him, though, no matter the tensile sexuality he wore like armor. Gisella took male admiration for granted and used it.

Rozalia had never presumed men were genuinely attracted to her. Too many had tried to use her as a stepping-stone to get to Gisella. It wasn't Gisella's fault that she was a beacon and Rozalia a fence post, but being overlooked left a mark, every time.

That's why she was confused by Viktor's sudden desire to dine with her. She was quite sure she had been the only one affected in the back of the car earlier, but he'd made this invitation sound vaguely sexual. If he was the least bit interested in her, it was only because she was here. Convenient. He had a reputation as a playboy and she had enough experience with players to recognize them.

What she didn't have experience with was feeling so drawn in by one.

She moved her gaze to the paintings before she started acting besotted again. She was confronted by a cheeky nude—literally a gathering of young women in a walled garden showing their backsides to the viewer. The rest were serene seascapes, fruit bowls, and peasants haying a field.

"You mentioned your grandmother dealt in art? I don't recognize these, but they're obviously masterpieces."

"My father was her only child. My mother pilfered everything from his family estate and brought it here. Her mother was next in line after Istvan. There was no one else to inherit this house." He paused, daring her to contest that.

Rozi wasn't here to make claims for Gisella's mother, only asked, "Is the furniture reproduction? Or originals?"

"Both. Our most heavily used is reproduction."

She noted the escritoire that was likely an authentic Louis Quinze. "I'm a nut for tiny drawers and hidden compartments," she admitted, firmly grasping her hands behind her back as she examined it. "I'm going to let myself believe there's a key to a secret passage in one of these."

"We had to lock it. To keep the ghosts from haunting the rest of the house."

After an exaggerated gasp of delight, she said, *"Thank you."*

His mouth twitched, but their drinks arrived before she could coax any more humor out of him than that one dry comment.

As they took their drinks, she made herself meet his gaze, no matter how disturbing, and say, *"Egészségére."*

He repeated it and they sipped.

"Is it too bold to ask you to tour me around?" she asked.

"You wish to case the place?"

"No." Was he serious or joking? So hard to tell. "I'm an artist. I'm interested."

"That's a lot of hats. I thought you were a gemologist and a goldsmith."

"I'm midway through a master of fine arts in metalwork and jewelry design." Did she take satisfaction from the slight elevation of surprise in his brows? Heck, yes, she did. "I work full-time for my uncle, making custom jewelry he sells in the shop my grandfather started. Barsi on Fifth? It's quite well-known in New York."

It might not have been featured in the title of a movie, but it held a similar reputation and was frequented by the same upper-class clientele.

"I know who your uncle is," he said blithely.

"Then you know he wouldn't hire me on nepotism alone. He expects me to constantly fill the well, which is why I'm continuing my education. But all art is inspiration for my own work. I would hate to miss this opportunity to study the masters who came before me, even though their disciplines are different from my own."

He cocked his head in a small nod, relenting, and waved toward the hall where they had entered. He took her first to a music room where the brass pipes of an organ reached toward the sixteen-foot ceilings. A wall of double doors opened into the adjacent ballroom, which was straight out of *Beauty and the Beast*.

"Wow."

"In answer to your earlier question, we host charity events and the odd film crew shooting a period piece."

"I love those." She moved into the center of the parquet floor and turned a slow circle, taking in the white walls with gilded trim, blue velvet curtains over the leaded windows and the chandeliers dripping with crystal. "What a dizzying place to live."

"It's an expensive obligation. I'd be fine with a modest apartment."

She bet his definition of *modest* was a lot different from the place she occupied. Even so, this was only one of his many homes. What were the rest like?

"I'm a romantic, I'm afraid," she confessed as he led her out to a hallway of portraits and vases that were so colorful and ornate they should have been gaudy but were perfectly tasteful in this surrounding. There was a chill in the air, though, and a faint scent of disuse. "I never want to hear that it's actually cold as Hades to live here, even in summer. Or that back in the day, they had to use outhouses and drank bad water."

"Mmm. I don't know whether you'll be pleased with this room or not, then." He took her into an enormous dining room. It was very stately and beautiful, but distinctly chilly and empty. It held only a circular table with eight chairs upon an enormous rug. The windows looked on to the front grounds. "There's a compartment in the floor where a table for forty is kept. At different times, people have hidden there."

"Like you? Playing hide-and-seek when you were young?" She came from a big, lively family, but recalled at the last second that he had lost his only sibling, an older brother, when they'd been young men.

"Or you meant in wartime?" she hurried to add, trying to smooth over her gaffe.

"Both of those." His expression remained inscrutable. "And the odd lover."

"Oh, I do enjoy hearing about skeletons in the family closet," she said with relish.

"Never found one of those. They always seemed to get out." He sipped the drink he carried.

She chuckled, more out of relief since his dry sense of humor gave her the impression he was relaxing a fraction. Not that she would call him affable. Not ever and certainly not to his face.

"They must be a consequence of arranged marriages. Lovers, I mean." She was teasing him a little, but also wondering if he really planned to succumb to such a thing.

"A consequence of being human, I'd say." He wasn't standing that close, but she suddenly felt the heat of his body. The lazy half-lidded look he gave her made her pulse thrum in her throat.

Would *he* resort to that? she wondered. If he succumbed to an arranged marriage?

She pushed the rim of her glass against her unsteady mouth, wondering what he would think if she told him she was a virgin at twenty-four. That she had made a pact at thirteen with her cousin to wait until they found a man they could truly love. It had partly been inspired their grandmother's great love for Istvan, but for Rozalia, it was more personal. She needed to be sure she gave herself to a man who wasn't secretly wishing she was Gisella.

"You come from a love match, I presume?" he asked, leading her into a smaller breakfast room that had a view of the back garden. It was still a showpiece, but much warmer and lived-in with fresh flowers and cut-crystal salt and pepper shakers on the lace tablecloth.

"My parents are deliriously in love," she said with a grin of affection, moving to the windows that likely caught the morning sun, making for a relaxed start to the day. "But I will concede such a thing to be impractical." She threw that over her shoulder, then tilted her head to reconsider her words. "Actually, my parents are impractical people, so I don't know if one correlates to the other."

"Impractical how?" He came to stand next to her and pointed out the window to the hexagonal windows that formed the roof of a squat, round building. "Like that sort of folly?"

"Why is it a folly? What is it?"

"A conservatory. My mother insists the staff keep it up, even though we can buy orchids for a fraction of the cost of heating that monster."

"May I see inside it?"

He drew her into a hall where casual jackets hung over a boot bench, then opened the door she suspected was referred to as the service entrance. Faint kitchen noises came from behind a closed door. Looking along as she went down the outside steps, she saw a formal veranda obscured by a privacy hedge.

He was showing her the "home" part of his house, which gave her a sense of privilege and made her warm to him even though he remained very aloof.

Cool evening air surrounded them as they crossed to the

door of the conservatory. She hugged her arms across her chest, hiding the way her nipples pushed against the fabric of her T-shirt, glancing nervously to see he'd noticed.

If anything, his attention made her nerve endings tingle all the harder, becoming even more sensitized and receptive. She had never reacted so elementally to any man before in her life. She kept wondering if this was how her grandmother had felt around Istvan—enthralled and ensnared. Helpless to powerful attraction. Desperate, even. *Like me, want me.* She didn't want to be that needy, ever, but couldn't hide from herself that he stoked that compulsion in her.

They entered the conservatory. It was humid as the tropics in here. She inhaled the earthy, dank undertones layered with heady floral aromas and a fragrance of citrus and herbs.

"I love the smell."

His nostrils twitched and his chest expanded. He grew pensive. "I haven't been in here for years."

"I would be in here every day if it was mine." She looked to the glass ceiling partially obscured by the fat leaves of exotic jungle plants. "This must be amazing in the winter. Oh, butterflies! How magical. You really are the luckiest person to have this."

"There were birds once. Tomatoes were protected in that section and berries there." He pointed to some cold frames. "My brother and I got into them. Left the doors open. The birds got into the berries and the cat got after the birds. We were banned after that."

She smiled, heart squeezed by the memory. It sounded so beautifully human. She wanted to hear more, but his expression stiffened and closed up as though he regretted sharing.

"We grew a garden every summer," she said. "My

mother always put up her own preserves—even though you can buy canned peaches off the shelf for half the price." She teasingly threw his words back at him.

"She didn't work?"

"She had four children. It was work, trust me." She rubbed a sage leaf and dipped her head to draw in the scent. "But being a stay-at-home mother was her dream. She was a daughter of immigrants and grew up in the back of the jewelry shop, mostly raised by her half sister—Istvan's daughter Alisz."

She copied his beat of silence, offering him a moment to argue that while sending him a look that told him he'd have an argument on his hands if he did.

He only lifted an unimpressed brow, not intimidated in the least.

She licked her lips and continued.

"Mom wanted to give us what she felt she had missed. She even day-cared Gisella. Mom didn't take any money for it, either. Even though Aunt Alisz would have paid a nanny so she wanted to pay Mom. Even though we could have used the money. That's what I mean about my parents being impractical. My mom viewed caring for her sister's child as simply what you do for family. Maybe it was even payback for Alisz watching her when she was little. But Aunt Alisz didn't have to work. Her ex-husband is quite well-off. Aunt Alisz wanted to pursue her academic career, though. My mom supported her aspiration by looking after her daughter."

The way he looked at her, eyes narrowed as he weighed and measured all her words, made her wonder if she should repeat it in Hungarian.

"What does your father do?" he asked.

"He runs a nonprofit office that finds housing for the homeless."

"It sounds as though you come by your romantic streak honestly."

"I really do. 'Pursue your dreams and you'll never work a day in your life' is the family motto."

"Dreams don't fill stomachs."

"Tell me about it. But we're not completely without sense. My older brother is a volcanologist. A wanderer, but gainfully employed at least some of the time. My younger brother swims. He still lives at home, but he's training for the Olympics. That's a full-time job in itself. Our baby sister, Bea, has applied to Juilliard for dance and she's also very talented, so why shouldn't we encourage her?"

Rozi leaned in to smell a lily. As the heady perfume filled her nostrils, velvet grazed her nose. She jerked back. "I always do that. Do I have pollen on my nose now?"

He brushed his fingertip against the tip of her nose.

Such a jolt of electricity went through her, she drew back sharply, tucking her chin and touching the spot herself to soothe the lingering burn. A myriad of feelings swirled through her. Self-consciousness, sheepish amusement, something uncertain and shy as she reacted to the most innocuous of caresses from him.

Did he think her horribly gauche?

He wasn't laughing. His shrewd gaze seemed to delve all the way to her soul.

"And you chose to keep a foot on each side, artistry that is also a practical trade."

A warm glow suffused her at words that weren't even a compliment, but so few people *saw* her. She was the forgotten middle child, the one who mediated and pleased and stepped back to let the leaders and the babies have the spotlight.

"My vocation chose me. Partly it was growing up around the family business. My mother used to leave Gizi and me at the shop while she ran her errands. I never wanted to go anywhere else. And my parents always encouraged me to go after my dream. What if they had told me to get a business degree? I'd be miserable."

"I have a business degree."

"Do you enjoy what you do?"

"I enjoy my standard of living," he said dryly. "I don't need to paint or sculpt to feel fulfilled. It's enough to watch the stock numbers go up and know that my decisions, and whatever risks I've taken lately, have paid off."

"I'm not much of a risk-taker."

"Aren't you?"

She really wasn't, but he had a point. In the back of her head, she could hear her mother freaking out that she was alone with a stranger in a faraway city, putting herself in a precarious situation in a stone-walled hothouse where no one would hear her screams.

But the risk Viktor posed had nothing to do with murdering her and hiding her body under the floorboards of his dining room. Her entire body was still tingling from the brush of his fingertip against her nose. He made her think and want and wonder. She wasn't a covetous person. In her childhood, yes, she had been jealous of Gisella's electronics and pretty clothes and constant vacations to amusement parks, but she also knew that she was very lucky. Gisella's parents had divorced. Gisella envied Rozalia's jumble of family and her affectionate parents and the fact Rozi *wasn't* pursued by every man who walked by.

So Rozi wasn't eyeing up this man's circumstance beyond admiring the sheer beauty of him and everything around him. She wasn't drawn to him because he was six-foot-gorgeous. She was feeling, for once, like she was her own person. One who wished this intriguing man might find her halfway as interesting as she found him. She wanted to get to know *him*.

Which was a huge risk because she knew when she was out of her league and, seriously, she had only read about the sort of home runs he no doubt cracked out on a nightly basis.

But as he picked a pale pink hibiscus flower and tucked it behind her ear, she knew she was going to take a small risk and see where this would go. It was another opportunity she refused to miss.

Rozalia's lashes swept down shyly as he settled the flower behind her ear. He took the liberty of smoothing her hair over it, allowing his touch to linger against the fine, soft tails.

He reminded himself that seeming innocents could hide secrets. They could betray. She had already coaxed him into betraying himself, mentioning his brother, Kristof, when he had bricked off those painful memories never planning to revisit them. Ever.

This woman was definitely more threatening than she appeared. On the surface she was mousy, but her brown hair had streaks of caramel, her brown eyes glints of bronze and gold. She had an unerring sense of artistry, taking time to study pieces that were not the most eye-catching, but which he knew to be of the most esteemed works they possessed. She was tactile and curious, impulsively touching and smelling, but in a way that savored the experience.

She was fascinating to watch, making the mundane corners of his world new and interesting to him again. It made the idea of kissing her, of seeing how she would take in *that* experience, a compulsion he couldn't resist.

He touched her chin, urging her to lift her mouth. The

tip of her tongue appeared to wet them. His skin tightened. He lowered his head, not usually one to hesitate, but this was a one-time thing. He would never see her again after tonight. He would never kiss her *for the first time* ever again. It made him want to play and tease and draw this out.

He grazed his lips against hers until his own burned with anticipation. A small gasp parted her lips and she opened her eyes. Her pupils were massive, and the light changed around him, telling him his own were reacting. All of him was expanding in an urge to overwhelm but he only kept that one finger crooked under her chin, wanting the full impact to be this, just this. A kiss.

He settled his mouth more firmly over hers, felt the tremble of her soft, soft lips. The timid response as he took his time rocking to find the perfect fit. She lifted on her toes to increase the pressure and her lips clung to his.

A noise he didn't consciously make growled in his throat. He moved his hand to the side of her neck so her pulse pounded against the heel of his palm, and gave himself more freedom. He explored the silky shape of her lips from the pillowy softness of her bottom lip to the luscious curve of her top lip.

Then he tasted her. Deeply.

And she moaned. Deeply.

He was dimly aware of her hands splaying against his ribs, nails like kitten claws as she searched for balance while rising higher on her toes, wanting more.

Sliding his arm around her slender waist to support her, he pulled her in. Her one arm came up around his neck and the warm swells of her breasts mashed into his chest. She softened in surrender, unleashing the barbarian in him.

He dug his hand into the thick silk of her hair and plundered. Made love to her mouth and filled his hand with the lush cheek of her behind. Pulled her up so she could feel his growing arousal straining against her mound.

She dove her fingers into his hair and encouraged him. Sucked delicately on his tongue while shyly dallying her own across it. It was both carnal and sweet. He forgot everything except that this woman ought to be his. He wanted to take her to the gravel at their feet and make it happen. He also wanted to stand here and savor the most flagrantly passionate kiss he'd ever experienced. The most purely sensual woman he'd ever met.

As he started to guide her leg up to curl her knee at his hip, her other foot turned. She gasped and grasped at him. He had a firm hold on her and it only took a half step to regain their balance, but it was enough to pull them out of their sexual spiral.

Her expression was stunned. His heart was pounding, his breath uneven.

"That—" She carefully drew back until she stood before him without so much as a loose thread connecting them. Her shaking hand went to her mouth. "That wasn't what I came here for," she said in a voice still husky with desire.

The earring, he recalled, and felt his lip curl with bitter knowledge. Because even women who gave up sweet, passionate kisses could have ulterior motives.

CHAPTER THREE

THEY DINED ON the formal veranda, overlooking the walled grounds. Heat lamps took the chill off the air and added a pinkish glow to the candlelight against the white tablecloth. Frogs croaked in the pond over the subtle violin humming sweetly from unseen speakers. The only evidence of the city that surrounded them was the sky staying indigo so the stars remained faint, rather than twinkling against an ink-black sky.

It would have been even more fairy-tale perfection if a block of tension hadn't fallen between her and her host.

She had wanted him to kiss her, to see how it would feel, but who could expect such a rolling wildfire? It had raced through her, blanking her to everything except the primal flex of his shoulders and neck, his raw, masculine scent and the lingering taste of alcohol on his tongue.

They had barely spoken in the twenty minutes since, but her butt still felt the imprint of his hand. The intimacy of kissing him refused to be forgotten as she set delicate morsels of duck soaked in orange liqueur into her mouth and chased them with a shred of clove-spiced beet and a sip of a full-bodied red wine.

It wasn't like that had been her first kiss, for heaven's sake. She was technically a virgin, but she'd had a couple of boyfriends. She had fooled around with them. None of that intimate wrestling had ever made her feel even close to the way she had felt with Viktor's finger under her chin, though. His arm going around her had seemed to draw her into a different dimension from the world she had always occupied.

She had thought she was a mature, independent adult, but as she contemplated kissing him again, she felt as though she stood in the narrow space between the girl she had been and the woman she was about to become. Not that she thought one sex act could be the marker into maturity. No, it was more than that. She instinctively knew making love with him would be more than simply a sex act.

Her pact with Gisella drifted through her mind, but she was already thinking, *This is different, Gizi.* So different. She didn't know how to explain it, but Viktor wasn't the same as the men she had dated—the ones she had thought seemed nice so she had given them a chance. The ones whose kisses were like digestive biscuits and their touches clumsy as a dog's nose going where it wasn't wanted.

The ones who lusted after her cousin on sight, forgetting all about *her.*

Viktor's kiss had been dark chocolate and whipped cream and bold, intoxicating red wine. His touch had been full of promise to lead her unerringly into the most exotic, spectacular and satisfying places.

She had always thought the word *attraction* meant that something or someone was appealing, but now she understood true attraction was a genuine *magnetism.* Viktor pulled her in a way she couldn't fight even if she wanted to.

She didn't want to. That was what shocked her. She wasn't the one-nighter type, but she was sitting here contemplating a one-night stand with him. It wasn't seduction on his part or even the spell of her surroundings. It was *him.*

It was the uniqueness of her reaction to him.

"Why is the earring so important to you?" he asked, breaking the silence.

It wasn't, she realized with an almost visceral *thunk* of realization inside her. The earring was the furthest thing from her consciousness right now.

She sipped her wine to wet her throat. "From the time Gisella and I heard the story of them, it's been our quest to find them and return them to our grandmother."

"And the story you heard is that Istvan gave them to her." Viktor's brow went up with skepticism.

"As an engagement promise, yes. He told Grandmamma to sell the first one to get away from the unrest. He promised to meet her in America but was killed in the demonstrations before he could join her. When she ran out of money from the first earring, she went to the man who became my grandfather, Benedek Barsi. Rather than buy it from her, he asked her to marry him. He sold the earring to open the shop."

"Such a fickle heart."

"She loved Istvan very much!" Tears had come into her grandmother's eyes every time she'd ever spoken of him. "But she was a single mother alone in a new country. They needed each other."

"So they agreed to the sort of arrangement that you find so archaic. You understand that without a blood test, there's no reason for me to believe your cousin is a Karolyi descendant? Perhaps this story was simply a pretty tale spun for a pair of curious little girls."

She shook her head, wondering how she could feel so drawn to someone who possessed this much cynicism.

"There's too much grief in her when she speaks of him." Not that she'd asked her grandmother about it recently. She couldn't even recall why Grandmamma had talked about it initially. It had been after Grandpapa's passing. Somehow Gisella had learned that she didn't actually share a grandfather with Rozalia. In their shock, they had asked Grandmamma about it and the tale had fed Rozalia's hunger for stories of grand passion.

But her grandmother's sadness had been real.

"I'll message Gizi later, ask her to do a blood test. I don't know why I didn't think of that. I guess I took my grandmother's word for it."

His faint smile dismissed her as naive.

She frowned. "Why would she pick a man of your greatuncle's stature to claim as the father of her child?"

"To make a claim against our fortune?" he suggested dryly.

"We're not making one. I came to make a fair and legitimate offer for the earring. All I want is for my grandmother to hold again the token given to her by her first love."

"Does she want that?"

"Why wouldn't she?"

"Perhaps she doesn't possess your level of sentimentality."

"What's wrong with being sentimental? Do you not have any special fondness for some place or thing? A sense of nostalgia for eating berries with your brother?" She nodded toward the conservatory.

His expression hardened, warning her she was treading dangerous ground.

She wasn't trying to upset him, only demonstrate what she knew to be true.

"An object doesn't have to be something of high value," she continued. "Or even something that can be quantified. I could work anywhere, but I choose to work in the family shop. Part of it is loyalty to family. And yes, my uncle provided my apprenticeship so I owe him for that, but I could have pursued other placements. I want to work in that particular shop because that place is special to me. I don't care where I live so long as I can go there every day. It's my *real* home."

He wasn't impressed. She could see it in the flat lines of his expression.

"Okay, try this, then. It's like when I ordered *pálinka* earlier. It gave me a taste of home, which helps me feel the strength of my family behind me."

"Why did you need that?" His gaze sharpened.

"Because this is overwhelming! I've never traveled so far on my own. Never met anyone like you or experienced a place like this. Don't you like to feel your family at your back sometimes?"

His mouth twitched. "I have a mother and a great-aunt. I stand at their back."

She blinked in astonishment. "But—" She stopped herself from asking, *What about when you lost your brother?* "They're your only family? You should definitely meet Aunt Alisz and Gisella, then."

"So I might have more responsibility? Unnecessary," he dismissed.

"So you have more family."

"They're not my family," he dismissed further. "Even if we do share DNA. You really are a romantic."

Yes, they are, she wanted to argue. She could tell he wasn't willing to see it that way, however.

"So you don't have any emotional connections to…anything?"

"My emotions are basic. I prefer physical comfort over being too hot or cold. I like good food and the satisfaction of achieving goals. Sometimes I enjoy watching sport finals or fishing off my yacht. I like sex," he said with such a direct look, it was an arrow into her heart. "But I have no desire for the drama of love affairs and tasting death to prove I'm alive or other nonsense like that."

"Nonsense," she repeated with a little choke. "If you knew how much you sound like my aunt Alisz, who sees no value in playing and having fun, you wouldn't be able to deny that you're related to her." But her aunt's notoriously blunt and aloof personality was a story for another day. She straightened in her chair. Drew a breath. "If you have no attachment to the earring, why don't you sell it to me?"

"Because I don't want you to have it." He spoke like he was addressing a child. "Your grandmother stole it. She profited well off her theft. I'm still astounded you have the gall to come here and ask me for it." He took a sip of wine, steady as a rock. "But I'm not impassioned with anger over it. Merely displeased."

She had to wonder what *would* provoke him to impassioned anger.

"Will you show it to me?"

"I'm still thinking about that."

"All right, fine," she said, throwing her napkin beside her plate. "Let's remove sentiment and allow me to argue on an intellectual level. As a man who occasionally likes to fish, I presume you have an interest in all the latest rods and flies—"

His expression didn't change, but she heard the pun as soon as he did. Rods. Flies. They were right back to the ball joke.

"Stop it. I'm saying that if you had an opportunity to view unique equipment—"

He sipped, maybe to hide his smile. "I assume comedienne is another of your many professions."

"You know what I'm driving at," she said with exasperation. "From what I've been told, the craftsmanship in the earring is rare and remarkable. I've seen one mediocre catalogue photo of it. It may not sway you that I would consider holding it as an honor and a privilege, but I hope you would be willing to satisfy my curiosity. As an artist," she tacked on, self-conscious now, especially because the corners of his mouth were digging in.

"If nothing else, Ms. Toth, you are entertaining."

"Allow me to give you my professional, educated opinion on the earring and I'm sure I can come up with a few more risqué innuendos while I'm at it."

"I have no doubt." He was sitting back in his chair, relaxed, and threw back the last of his wine, then set aside his glass decisively. "Very well. Let's go to my office."

"Really?" Her heart nearly came out her throat.

"Perhaps you'll tell me it's a fake and we're arguing over nothing."

He led her to a study next to the receiving parlor. It held the smell of the ashes in the unlit fireplace and leather-bound books. The books were free of dust and arranged in severe lines on a wall of shelves. There was a door to the parlor and a small footstool to the side of the desk, closest the windows. Its placement gave her the impression he often swiveled his chair to set his feet there and contemplate his kingdom through the windows.

Over the marble mantel, an imposing portrait stared down at the pair of leather chairs that faced the desk.

"Is that your father?" The clothing didn't seem right, but the resemblance to Viktor was undeniable.

"Istvan."

Oh. No wonder her grandmother had fallen so hard. He seemed to project Viktor's same aloof confidence.

"And this is Cili." Viktor went behind the desk, drawing her gaze to the painting he pulled away from the wall to reveal the safe mounted behind it.

Rozi moved so she could get a better look at the seated

woman wearing a yellow gown with a billowing skirt. She cradled a dog in her lap. The work captured beautifully the glint of light against satin and the hues in the dog's fur.

"There's no combination. It's my fingerprint. You can't break in unless you plan to dismember me."

"I'm looking at her, wondering how people sat for so long in those days. Surely that dog got fed up and snapped at her? But she keeps that peaceful smile on her face."

He closed the safe and swung the painting back into place. "The painter was her lover."

"Of the dining room floorboard lovers?"

"He didn't carve his initials into the space, so we can only assume he spent time there. Her marriage was arranged, and despite her husband's generous wedding gift of a pair of elegant earrings, their relationship was strained. That's why my aunt Bella was allowed to forgo marriage. Her mother refused to trap her in a situation she adamantly opposed."

"She never married?"

"Her romantic feelings lay in a direction that was considered inappropriate. She's had companions over the years. She lives alone now."

"But your mother was persuaded to marry your father when your grandmother offered the earring she'd managed to recover."

"This one, yes." He opened a velvet box and showed her the clover of sapphires and diamonds set in granulated gold nestled on a bed of satin.

She gasped aloud, shocked by the visceral impact of seeing it for the first time. Her gaze ate up the square-cut blue sapphires and dozens of tiny diamonds, maybe a twentieth of a carat, that formed the petal patterns around the oval sapphire in the center. A gem hung from the bottom, framed in more of the intricate beadwork.

Emotive tears sprang to her eyes—the kind that over-took a marathon runner in the last sprint. She couldn't even touch it. Could only hold her hands to her cheeks as she gazed, transfixed.

Had he expected more avarice? Yes. Instead, she wore a look of reverence. She had said she would consider hold-ing the earring an honor and a privilege. He had thought she was exaggerating. He hadn't even understood the con-cept since he had never been humbled by anything. Not by an object and certainly not by a person—the painful situation around his brother's death notwithstanding. Re-sponsibility had tested his mettle, of course, forcing him to prove what he was made of, but that didn't intimidate him. He had risen to that challenge, refusing to let it make him feel small.

He had never looked on something as she did right now, as though grateful to be in the presence of something be-yond her.

"What are you seeing that I don't?" he asked, glanc-ing at the bauble. "It's eye-catching, I suppose, but the assessed value isn't that high. It's twenty-two karats. The stones are decent. Hand-cut, but not of a particularly rare quality. When it comes to sapphires, the pink ones are more valuable."

"It's the workmanship. The artistry. The wedding an-nouncement said the violet blue of the stones matched her eyes." She glanced at the painting, then touched her fin-gers over his, tilting the box. "Do you have a loupe? Four times twelve plus…"

"Eighty diamonds, ten sapphires. There are smaller sap-phires here."

"All bezel set," she murmured. "Pulling the stones would mean melting this down afterward, but look at this

granulation. That was a very tricky process at the time."
She launched into talk of Etruscan artifacts and how the
effect was thought at first to be achieved with stamps and
that ancient charcoal fires had unreliable temperatures.
"The ancient Greeks were soldering these beads in place
with a mixture they created by heating salt-coated cop-
per plates with potash, soap and lard. How does someone
even figure out a chemical reaction like that?"

Indeed. Chemistry was a mystery.

He watched more than listened as a kaleidoscope of
emotions crossed her expression while she spoke. Awe
and enthusiasm, discovery and sorrow at the tiny dent of a
granule, as if the piece was a baby bird with a broken wing.

"The earrings only exist because Fulop tolerated the
Soviet elite," he told her. "He held dinners in their honor
so he could keep this." He waved at the ceiling and walls.
"Cili wore them for all social occasions. She was famous
for them. That's why their disappearance was so notable."

"What if Istvan did give them to my grandmother,
though?" Her gaze came up, not pressing her case. More
an investigation driven by curiosity.

"Stole them from his own mother?"

"Istvan was a student demonstrator, wasn't he? Against
the Soviets? He must have had a rebellious streak."

"That was your grandmother's influence."

"Is that what you were told? That he was led astray by
her? I heard it the other way around. He was angry with
his father for cooperating with the enemy. Grandmamma
was terrified for him and wanted him to stop going to the
protests. She fell in love with his passion, but worried as
the crackdowns began that he was taking undue risks." She
dropped her touch from his hand, chin coming up. "How
does your understanding of her motive even make sense?
You think she singled out a student from a rich family and

enticed him to demonstrate so she could steal his mother's earrings? How?"

He set the earring on the side of his desk, then met the spark of challenge flaring in her eyes. "I believe she aspired to marry a rich student. She likely influenced him with her proletariat politics."

"Influenced him how? By showing herself to be of the poor and struggling class? Perhaps he was moved by her plight. She was pregnant. Maybe he wanted a better future for his child."

"We don't know that baby was his."

"Why would my grandmother make that up?"

"We could debate this all night, but we have no way of arriving at the truth until your cousin takes a blood test." He was convinced he had been in possession of the truth for years anyway.

Her mouth pouted. "I don't like you thinking badly of my grandmother."

"We're strangers. What does it matter what I think? Ah," he said as she bit her lip in consternation. "You're concerned what I think of *you*."

She shrugged, admitting reluctantly, "True. And I'm not sure why." Her brows came together in dismay. "You're not the sort of man whose attention I typically want or expect to earn."

"What sort of man is that?"

"One who's used to getting whatever he wants. One who's not serious." There was rebuke in her doe eyes.

"I assure you, I'm a very serious man."

They were talking about different types of serious, but his remark didn't intimidate her. It made a smile play around her mouth, as though she was amused. He should have been affronted but found that smile entrancing.

"I think you're different from the women I normally

spend time with. You're playful. Impulsive. Definitely more sensual than anyone I've ever encountered." He noted where her fingers were tracing the brocade upholstery on the back of a chair, learning its texture. "I find that quality in you very intriguing. I think that, after such a passionate kiss, I would like to know if you respond like that during lovemaking."

So would I, Rozi found herself thinking with a semihysterical laugh bubbling in her chest.

"Um—" She felt buffeted by winds that swept all rational thought from her mind. "That's not my usual MO."

In fact, it was one reason she didn't seem to keep boyfriends. In this day and age, they expected to go all the way after a few dates. She always drew a halt because she had never felt strongly enough about any of them, emotionally or physically, to abandon her pact with Gizi.

No one had ever made her feel like *this*, though.

As Viktor's attention stayed on her mouth, Rozalia couldn't think of anything but the strange, wild kiss they'd shared. Of tasting him again. Something urgent battled past her conscious reasoning. It was the insistent part of her that overtook her when she was in the heat of design work, expressing the very core of herself with precious metals and rare stones.

She didn't have the tools and skills for lovemaking, though. She only had instinct and a deep longing to succumb to that brilliant force. It had never let her down, always saturating her with the deepest joy and leaving her with a sense of fulfillment.

So she put her trust in it. She stepped close and put out her hand so her palm rested on his chest where his heartbeat thumped strong and hard. She knew it was an invitation, a signal to begin. Her own pulse filled her ears with an echoing throb, pushing sensual heat through her limbs and into her erogenous zones.

He made a noise that was feline and satisfied, predatory but lazy. Almost a purr, yet a growl, too. Warning and welcoming as he drew her in with firm hands on her hips.

She gasped at the hardness of his frame, the confidence in his hands, the languorous way he nuzzled his nose against hers for one teasing second. It was a gentle urging to tilt her head so he could capture her mouth more surely. Thoroughly.

Sensation slammed through her as he picked up right where they'd left off, the rush so intense it *hurt*. Her nerve endings stung as though electrified. Her breasts grew full and tender, her lips became plump and sensitized. Her muscles ached with the effort to hold on to him when she felt weak, weak, weak. Her throat constricted with emotion and her lungs burned for oxygen. Deep between her legs, a pulsation of need started.

All from a kiss. From the sweet rough rake of his mouth across hers. A swipe of ownership, yes, but of enticement. *Come with me. Let me show you.*

He drew back, a question in his eyes as he took her hand.

She let him draw her from the office and up the stairs. Crazy, crazy, crazy. But she had come this far. Why not go all the way?

All the way down the gallery to a room with double doors, a sitting room with a desk, then through another pair of doors into a room with an enormous bed. Bigger than a king, she thought vaguely. Because he was more man than even that title could convey. More man than any sort of person she had ever encountered.

The drapes were already shut and a lamp lit. He closed

the doors. Locked them with a click that gave her the slightest pause.

Then he came across and touched her again. He pulled her into a gentle collision that melted her on contact. So much seductive heat. Even his eyes glowed feverishly bright.

That was what really affected her—his desire. The hardness of his muscled shoulders and chest triggered primal responses of female to male, but her delicate feminine ego exalted in the specific hardness that pressed insistently against the softness of her belly. She reveled in the color that flagged his cheekbones. In the tension that pulled at his expression, indicating a struggle with his control.

She wound her arms around his neck and gave herself up to that force. To him.

He took her mouth. Took it as if this same energy inside her gripped him. As though this raw, aching hunger drove him to the same pitch. As if he needed her to match his need or they would both be lost.

It was overwhelming and wild and made her tremble, but she didn't even try to slow him down. She didn't care that she couldn't breathe. This was the beauty of abandonment.

Still, a dim part of her worried she wasn't as skillful a lover as he expected. Was she supposed to be more forward? Less? She *wanted* to feel more of him. Wanted to feel his skin. Did he grow impatient with her when she drew back to clumsily try to undo his buttons? Was that why he ran a firm hand down the center, dislodging buttons that stung as they sprang away and struck her arm and shoulder. He jerked his shirt open and yanked to free the tail.

She swallowed uncertainly, but her hands went to his hot, tawny chest, too hungry for the damp, satin feel of him to let doubt prevail.

He made that sexy growling noise and his own hands got under the edges of her T-shirt. They scorched her lower back and she jerked in reaction. He pressed her arms up as he peeled the shirt away in a trailing caress of his light hands, then drew hers behind his neck.

She wrapped her arms more securely around his neck, shuddering as his chest hair abraded the upper swells of her aching breasts. She couldn't get enough of the feel of him and licked up his throat in sheer wantonness.

Her bra released and he slid his tickling touch along her arms, forcing her to draw back so he could peel it off and throw it away.

He caught her before she could throw herself into his arms again. Caught her by the upper arms and held her before him as he looked.

She swallowed, told herself not to have body issues because—

"Oh!" His sure hands cupped her breasts, plumping them. Making them ache even as he soothed with gentle massage and light flicks of his thumbs across her nipples.

She shifted her feet, trying to keep her balance under the onslaught of sensations.

He lifted his gaze to hers, watching to ensure she liked it. She could barely hold that penetrating gaze. Not while waves of heady, dizzying desire rolled through her. Her lashes fluttered and a dangerous wild heat flared between her thighs. Flared and burned and condensed into a coal of glowing abject need. Into pressure and tension and such acute pleasure she had to cover his hands and make a pleading noise for him to stop.

"Let it happen," he commanded.

She shook her head. Couldn't. She needed to be in the safety of his arms and looped her arms around his neck again.

He caught her up with hard hands behind her thighs, so she instinctively twined her legs around his waist and her mouth was on a level with his.

She kissed him. Greedily. She did every lurid, raunchy thing she had been longing to do to that mouth. She swept her tongue against his, explored the wet heat and different textures of him. She scraped her teeth across his erotic bottom lip, then sucked on it with carnal recklessness.

On and on it went until the world upended. Suddenly she was on her back on the mattress, his weight pressing briefly before leaving her as he rose to his knees between hers. He yanked at the fly of her jeans, then stepped off the bed to pull them away.

She cycled her feet to help, even peeled off her sock and lifted her hips to throw away her ridiculously comfortable but unsexy short-short girl boxers.

He dispatched his own clothing as unceremoniously. As urgently. Then he came down alongside her and set a hard knee between hers while his hand stroked from the outside of her thigh, up her hip, to capture her breast again.

If she had thought the brush of his chest a stimulating experience, the whole body sensation of hips and thighs and stomach brushing against her own made her groan. He was so beautiful, too, not that he let her admire him. He bent to suck the nipple he had teased to staunch attention, making her cry out at the initial hot, wet sensation. He lifted away, blew softly, then did it again.

Teased and tortured, she rolled into him, unable to get close enough, hands skimming his back and sides, learning the shape of roped muscles and the silky texture of his chest hair and how sensitive his nipples were to the graze of her fingertips.

She didn't even know what she was doing, but he jerked

and looked up at her with a dangerous smile of approval and threat. Then he sucked her nipple again. Hard.

It was the most delicious payback. Her toes curled and golden threads of desire shot into her loins. She found herself crooking a knee to enjoy the abrasion of his thigh against the inside of her own, rubbing like kindling, stoking the fire between them.

He drew her half under him, his forearm beneath her neck, and took his time petting and caressing her breasts and waist and hip, her stomach and finally, finally, he cupped her mound.

She bit her lip. Closed her eyes tight as the exquisite pressure of his palm released a rush of dampness.

He made that noise again, the one that was so primal she knew this to be utterly natural. The way man and woman were meant to be. He rocked his hand where she yearned for… So much. A deeper touch. Something mysterious and necessary.

She bucked, instinct taking her over. She arched in response to the way he teased her. She offered her breasts. Her lips. Everything. All that she was.

He kissed her lightly and kept up that slow shifting pressure of his hand. As if he knew the build he was inciting would grow by increments yet keep her this side of the abyss. With light fingers, he parted and explored, keeping her on the precipice, toying with her and driving her insane.

The only thing she could think to do was return the favor. She slid her hand to the thick, implacable heat against her thigh. She took hold of pure magic and discovered a new world. Silk over steel. Velvet and a new, deeply ragged sound that rattled from his throat.

"Yes." His voice was whiskey-soaked and made her scalp tighten.

She knew logically what she was begging for, but she didn't *know*. The way his weight came over her was overwhelming. She didn't have second thoughts, per se, but she had a moment of stunned realization at what she was doing. As if she had leaped from an airplane without fully grasping she was a mile above the earth.

He guided the broad dome of his sex over the sensitive knot of nerves, throwing her back into that chasm of craving where she only needed more. More of him. Of whatever he could give her. And he gave it to her. The crest of his tip pressed into the slick heart of her. Pressed and stretched, thrusting deep with confidence—

She gasped at the catch and burn.

He lifted his head. Some of the haze left his eyes while a moment of comprehension struck his expression.

This was it. The mating act.

It was the mile-high view of existence. Soaring and dangerous, but such a moment of awe.

Perhaps he saw the same thing because his expression, having gone shocked and tense with sudden clarity, eased into tenderness. He cupped her cheek and kissed her with a taste of adoration on his lips.

Maybe it was her romantic soul turning something earthy and base into something exalted and beautiful, but they were in free fall. She wanted this to go on forever. This soft kiss and this intensely intimate, sharp penetration.

Then he moved. He withdrew and thrust gently as he watched her with a smoky gaze from beneath heavy eyelids.

The friction hurt, but his easy pace sent frissons of pleasure through her, too. Ones that incited a glow that redoubled and expanded. She curled her arms around him, her legs. Drew him in and moved with him. Urged him with ancient, primitive signals to move faster. Harder.

He used his hands. His teeth. Kissed and touched and nibbled and said things she should have understood, but she was far beyond the world of words. There was only this mindless place where writhing pleasure soaked her. Where she clung to his powerful body and only his fierce possession of her mattered. Where one tiny twist of her hips had him striking into her like lightning, making her lose her breath and turn molten even as his arms caged her.

He splintered with her, fusing them with alchemy and sorcery and elemental power for the rest of eternity.

CHAPTER FOUR

IT WASN'T UNTIL he reached to keep the condom on as he withdrew that he realized he hadn't worn one.

It sent a frozen splash through him, snapping him out of his postclimactic lethargy. *How?* He *always* wore one.

It was one more shock on top of the sheer power of his release. He fell onto his back, absorbing what had been a cataclysm. And had she been a *virgin*?

She had been everything he could ever want in a lover. Abandoned and responsive, irresistible as creamed honey. Before he'd even had her naked, the animal in him had known once wouldn't be enough. He had been both urgent and determined to savor. Then she had clasped him in her delicate fingers and all he could think was that he needed to be inside her.

Her gasp as he'd thrust had been one of surprise. Pain, maybe. His world had been so perfect in those dark, wet heartbeats, he had been stunned at having misjudged how ready she was. He had thought it would kill him to pull out.

But emotions he couldn't name had dawned across her lovely face. To call it "knowledge" was too biblical, but that was what he had felt, gazing on her. In that second, he had known her at the deepest level because he had been in the same state of wonder and magnificence.

In those sublime moments, urgency had left him. He

had exalted in every caress from then on. Every catch of her lobe in his teeth and every glorious whimper he wrung from her throat had become a part of him. He would have stayed within her for a thousand years, but her climax had triggered his. There hadn't been a cell of sense in his head at that point. Not a single glimmer of willpower or control.

Now, however, cogs were turning and mental connections were being made.

"You were a virgin," he said. "Does that mean you're not using birth control?"

"Hmm?" She turned her head.

They were sprawled sideways across the wrinkled covers, her body still rosy in the golden light. Her hair was loose and mussed, her cheeks pink, her lips dry until she ran her tongue around them, leaving them shiny. Her sooty lashes blinked and her fine brows quirked together.

"I'll have to take a morning-after pill."

"You will," he assured her, prickles of disenchantment and suspicion firmly dousing his afterglow. How had he been such a fool? He would have sworn he had conquered this weakness for a soft touch and a pretty smile.

"We wouldn't want to repeat history," she said with a flick of her gaze into his, inviting him to laugh with her.

"No. I wouldn't," he agreed without a single iota of humor. He refused to repeat his own history with a woman who had seemed enamored with him but had betrayed him in a most coldhearted way.

Thinking far more clearly now, he realized what she must have been vying for.

"Was this your attempt to trade for the earring? If so, I'm still not interested."

I'm still not interested.

"What? No!" A single, jagged choke hit her throat, too

coarse to be a laugh. Mostly a noise of disbelief. She was reeling from what she'd just done and he was asking—*accusing* her of— She sat up. "Are you serious right now?"

I'm a very serious man.

She had thought him so funny when he said that. He had taken her meaning as a sense of humor, which had tickled her because she'd thought he was saying it as a type of self-deprecating joke. But she had been saying she recognized him as the kind of man who charmed a woman into bed without offering any sort of future.

"You're twenty-three? Four?" he asked.

"Twenty-four." She knew better than to fall for a player. Sure he had some good moves, but that was because he *practiced*. Ugh. She wanted to bury her head in her arms, she was so appalled with herself.

"Most people lose their virginity a lot younger these days."

"So what? Are you suggesting there was something wrong with the way I behaved?" She blushed. It started as embarrassment but intensified as she wondered if he was judging *her* moves. She had let instinct guide her, but maybe she'd been clumsy and laughable. Her lungs grew so tight she could hardly draw air.

"I'm suggesting you obviously don't experiment so there must be some ulterior motive for you to give your virginity to me, a perfect stranger. You must want something."

A shared and remarkable experience, perhaps?

"Don't flatter yourself. You're not perfect." Physically, maybe, but, "Why are you being so insulting?" She climbed off the bed and searched out her clothes.

He came up on an elbow, his form as lovingly carved as an ancient statue, each muscle delineated across his chest and into his abs. His thighs were powerful, his—

She averted her eyes, but felt his gaze linger on the sway of her breasts as she bent to snatch up her bra. He had all the languorous arrogance of a sheikh with his harem girl.

Well, this one had fulfilled her purpose and was dismissing herself. She didn't even bother trying to find her missing sock.

"Answer my question," he demanded. "Why me? What did you hope to gain?"

"Well, there was an element of Why *not* you? But I seem to have answered that. You'll be getting a one-star review for your afterplay."

His whole demeanor turned to granite. "You want me to believe the romantic who remained a virgin until twenty-four suddenly decided to seek a brief, pleasurable encounter with a man she met hours ago?"

"I'm the one entitled to the outrage. *You* are the player and I can't *believe* I let you play me." She hopped to get herself into her jeans and closed the fly. When he didn't reply, she shot a look over her shoulder. "Not going to dispute that accusation?"

"Do you want me to take you to a pharmacy? Pay for the pill?"

"Such a gentleman. No thanks." If he offered her money right now, she would actually kill him. "There's one near my hotel. I'm perfectly fine." Not perfect *at all*.

"I'll call my driver to take you."

"Oh, don't bother." Swallowing back a lump, Rozalia hurried to finish dressing. *This* was why she had made that childish vow with Gizi, so she wouldn't have this shuddering avalanche of regret tumbling onto her in the aftermath of what had seemed to be a truly lovely experience.

"Don't be ridiculous. It's dark." He kept hold of the phone.

"I'm sure your gatekeeper will be happy to call me a cab." She felt so *stupid*!

He dialed and she heard him talking, but she was already slamming her way out of his life.

Viktor woke early with a splitting headache and a distinct lack of appetite, but the ambition that typically propelled him out of bed was in full force, laced with disgust that he'd shunned his responsibilities last night.

He showered again, even though he had showered directly after Rozalia left.

He should have felt relieved by her departure. Instead, he had made a futile effort to wash away guilt and tremendous self-contempt for succumbing to his libido, along with a lingering discontent he couldn't identify.

Had he wanted her on sight? Yes. But he hadn't *played* her. He didn't prey on women. He liked to think of himself as a generous lover, in bed and out, and they had seemed physically compatible.

So, was it possible she had simply been swept away, as he had?

Since when was he "swept away"? He was a grown man, not a youth of seventeen, slave to a pretty smile and a glimpse of cleavage. He should have sent Rozalia away rather than bring her up here. He should have attended to the endless work he had been mentally juggling when he had walked out of his building and allowed himself to be distracted by...

He didn't want to think of her. Didn't want to pick apart their evening yet again, trying to decide whether he had misjudged her. He would drown in another bottle and he'd had more than enough last night. After calling to the gate a second time and being assured she'd been dispatched safely to her hotel, he'd poured himself a drink and set about numbing this nameless thing that roiled inside him.

It was still there, nipping at his heels as he dressed and went down to his office. Why had she given herself to him? Her *virginity*? Why, why, why?

He decided to work a few hours here, where the quiet would give him time to recover from his hangover before he drove in to the office where he was always in demand, even on a weekend.

The housekeeper spotted him on his way into his office. *"Kávé?"* she offered.

He nodded, sending a bolt of dull pain hammering through his skull. He went directly to the drawer where he kept a supply of headache capsules and swallowed two dry, gaze moving sightlessly over the top of his desk while he began to prioritize his day.

Which was when he recalled that he hadn't put the earring away last night, before taking Rozalia upstairs.

It wasn't here on the desk where he'd left it. It wasn't on the floor or anywhere here in his office.

Why had she given herself to him?

He had his answer.

Rozalia woke to an imperative knock on her hotel room door.

She was dressed in yesterday's clothes, having thrown herself onto the bed when she arrived back at her hotel last night. She had proceeded to bawl out a heart that shouldn't feel so broken after such a trifling thing as falling into bed with a philanderer.

"Ms. Toth. This is the police. Open the door." The last was said more quietly, as though to someone else. It must have been the hotel manager because her door was opened before she'd even pulled herself off the bed.

"What's wrong?" Her mind leaped to her family. Why else would the police barge in on her this way except to deliver horrible news?

Two uniformed police entered, a man and a woman. One directed the manager to wait outside. "Sit," the male officer ordered her, nodding toward the chair. The female officer proceeded to go through her things.

"What are you doing? What's wrong?"

"Tell me about this earring that you were so interested in acquiring from Mr. Rohan," the male officer commanded.

Rozalia kept pinching herself, hoping to wake from this nightmare, but it only grew worse as the hours wore on. She was brought to a police station, fingerprinted and questioned a second time, and charged with stealing the earring from Viktor's home.

It didn't matter how many times she said that she had only collected her bag from the parlor on her way out. "Doesn't he have surveillance cameras? You can see I don't have it with my things."

They didn't care that her words came out in perfect Hungarian. It was as if they didn't hear them at all. They allowed her to stay in her rumpled T-shirt and jeans but took all the rest of her things.

They let her make one phone call and by then she was nearly at breaking point. In her state of supreme anxiety and without her contact list, she could only remember the number for the shop—which was useless. It was late in New York. Past midnight. Her uncle would be home, asleep. Or maybe he'd gone to Florida? She couldn't remember.

She couldn't call her parents. She had told Viktor they were impractical, which was an understatement. In an emergency, they reacted with emotion, not cool-headed logic. They would try to comfort her, but as for hiring her a lawyer, they wouldn't know how to make an international call, let alone find her legal representation. And they simply didn't have the sort of funds she would need for bail.

She tried what she thought was Gisella's number, getting a dark look from the officer supervising her. He acted as though he was doing her favor, allowing her a second attempt to reach someone. Cold fingers of helplessness kept stroking over her skin, pushing tears into the backs of her eyes.

A man answered and a lump of despair filled her throat. "Oh, God. I dialed the wrong number. I'm so sorry."

"Wait. Are you looking for Gisella? I'll get her."

Suddenly her cousin's voice was on the phone and Rozi was so relieved, she fell apart. Afterward, she couldn't recall anything she said. All that mattered was that Gisella had said, *I'm coming.*

She handed off the phone to the officer so Gisella could get the details she needed and buried her face in her hands.

"What do you mean she was *arrested*?" Viktor barked. Things had been going from bad to worse for hours. At this news, his temper wasn't just lost. It was abandoned with malice aforethought. *"Where the hell is she?"*

And how long had she been in a cell? It had been eight hours since he had discovered the earring missing. Eight hours in which he asked his housekeeper to call the police, to ask them to *question* Rozalia. He said to search her room if necessary and ensure she didn't leave the country until the earring was located.

He didn't ask them to *arrest* her.

Officers had come here, as well. They had taken Viktor's statement and dusted his desk for fingerprints. They had questioned his employees, all of whom were day staff, not the butler and chef and gatekeeper from last night. Those employees had been called in over the course of the hours-long investigation, which was when Viktor had learned that Trudi had stopped by last night.

"What the hell was she doing here?"

"She was on the visitor log as an expected guest. I let her through," the gatekeeper stammered, anxious to take Viktor to the gatehouse to prove it if necessary.

All Viktor had really needed to hear was that his mother had been the one to put Trudi's name on the list. He called Trudi, who started out very haughty, playing the injured party.

"Your mother told me she had been called out of town," Trudi said. "She thought you might like company for dinner. Apparently you'd already found some." Her piqued tone rankled.

Endre had tried to turn Trudi away, Viktor learned. Endre had told Trudi that Viktor was with a guest. On her insistence, Endre had gone upstairs and swore he left Trudi in the parlor only long enough to confirm that Viktor had retired for the night. Since he hadn't been sure if Rozalia was still there, he hadn't disturbed him.

But the door between Viktor's office and the parlor was unlocked. When Viktor questioned Trudi further, asking directly if she had seen the earring, there was a long pause.

"We're fingerprinting the area right now. If there's something you'd like to tell me, now would be the time," he growled, control hanging by a thread.

"I glanced into your office to see if you were there," she said offhandedly. "It seemed a rather valuable piece to leave lying about. I moved it into the drawer of the end table in the parlor."

Mischief. Childish malicious mischief.

"I don't care for games, Trudi. Or possessiveness, especially when it's so misplaced. Do not hang around Budapest for me," he said flatly and ended their call.

Their "budding relationship" was dead on the vine.

Now as he attempted to track down Rozalia, he was thinking Trudi had best not hang around this hemisphere. The manager of Rozalia's hotel was stammering with deference as he informed Viktor that he'd searched the room a second time himself, trying to return his valuable property. The police had taken her into custody when she'd refused to tell them where she'd hidden it, or to whom she'd sold it.

Viktor might actually *kill* Trudi for this.

He left for the station, placing a terse call to his lawyer to meet him there.

Rozalia was exhausted, emotionally and physically, but she didn't bother trying to sleep in the cell. She sat on the hard bench, muscles aching with tension, alert to every noise and shift of her cellmates while she tried to disguise her terror. She listened hard and held herself in a state of firm discipline. Gisella would come through for her. She just had to wait.

Finally, a guard came to the door and spoke her name. A lawyer was here for her.

It was such a harsh jolt against the invisible shell she had formed around herself, Rozalia shuddered. Her knees felt spongey as she stood, her head catching a rush of blood that made her sway and put out a hand to brace herself.

The cold bar she grasped sent a chill of foreboding into her heart. This might be just a meeting, she reminded herself, trying not to get her hopes up. Given the way things were going, this might be her home for a long time.

She was shown into a room that held three people in suits and one in uniform. One was a woman and Rozalia latched instinctively onto her. She projected empathy from behind an expression of tension.

No way would she look at *that* suit, the one tailored to *his* broad shoulders. The ones she'd clung to last night as if he could give her everything in the world. Everything she craved.

She swallowed a sour ache. That vile bastard was the reason she was here. If she dared allow herself a feeling right now, it would be pure hatred.

The woman introduced herself as Sophie Balogh.

"My cousin hired you?" Rozalia asked, voice husky from lack of use.

"Technically I've been retained by Kaine Michaels. I will bill him through our related firm in America, but yes, I'm here at Gisella Drummond's request."

Kaine Michaels? She didn't want Gisella in his debt because of her!

Some misguided instinct had her looking to *him* for one helpless second.

Viktor's gaze was waiting for her. His face was stiff and unreadable, but she could feel the fury radiating off him as he drilled through her confused gaze to catch fresh hooks into her heart.

"I didn't take it!" she blurted at him, even more anguished than she'd been last night when he'd accused her of wanting to trade herself for it.

"It's been located," he said tightly. "In my home."

"Then why am I here?" she cried, hands going into the air with helplessness.

Sophie inserted herself between them and touched Rozalia's arm, steadying her, insisting on gaining her attention. "Mr. Rohan has already made arrangements for your release."

Rozalia pulled into herself, hugged her ribs and held the woman's gaze.

"I want *you* to arrange it," she said through lips that felt numb, like she was drunk and the words in her head wouldn't form on her mouth. "I don't want to owe him. *I'll* pay you when it comes time. Don't involve Kaine Michaels."

"It's all done," Sophie said gently. "There are some documents to be filed and you may have to appear before a judge to fully expunge this incident, otherwise it could haunt you when you travel. I'm happy to take over that part of it, but either way, you are—" She sent a stern look toward the men. "More or less, free to go."

"What do you mean, 'more or less'?" Rozalia asked with panic.

Viktor still wore that intimidating look, as if he wanted to tear someone limb from limb.

"The hotel manager has seized this moment for his twenty minutes of fame," Viktor bit out. "Reporters have staked out your hotel. I've offered to take you—"

"I'd rather go back to a cell."

"Ms. Toth—" Both lawyers started to protest, but Viktor silenced the room by opening the door.

Calling her bluff? Rozalia almost burst into fresh tears at his coldhearted cruelty.

"Come," Viktor said with a sweep of his hand, voice grave. "I got you into this. Allow me to get you out."

Not sending her back to her cell, then.

"How?"

"I have a home in the mountains where no one will bother you."

Biting her lip, *refusing* to let it tremble, she walked ahead of him, turning in the direction of the exit. Toward fresh air and freedom.

They had to stop at the intake counter where her things were given back to her. She shakily went through her purse, ensuring her wallet and phone were there. Her phone was down to 20 percent and had about a hundred notifications on it, mostly from her mother. She was offered a pen to sign for everything and she started to scroll her signature, but—

"Where's my ring? They put it in an envelope." She started to scramble through her purse again, working through the hidden pockets. "I gave them my ring. They made me take it off and said I would get it back! Where is my ring?"

The man behind the counter shrugged stupidly and Viktor had the *gall* to touch her shoulders and say, "I'm sure it's here. Stay calm."

Calm? *Calm?*

She slapped him away and fisted her hands on the counter. "I was falsely arrested for stealing. I'm not going to become a victim to it. Find. My. Ring."

"Mind yourself," the officer behind the counter warned her.

Viktor tried to get in front of her while his own lawyer quickly stepped in front of both of them, urging everyone to keep their tempers.

A moment later, an envelope with her name on it was located and her ring tumbled from the corner where it had been caught.

Rozalia was shaking so hard she could hardly thread it onto her finger. Viktor tried to help but she batted him away again. She had her ring, her phone, and shouldered her purse. She was leaving.

* * *

Her eyes were sunken and bruised, her hair limp, her clothes rumpled and her mouth pouted with exhaustion. Her whole demeanor was one of furious anguish, but she had kept a cool head right up until the ring incident.

Do you not have any special fondness for some place or thing?

No. He hadn't cared about losing the actual earring when he discovered it missing. Not really. Thievery was infuriating in any form and the value of the earring was enough to grate, but he wasn't attached emotionally to the gold and stones.

The sense of betrayal had gone deep under his thick skin, though, along with the ignominy of allowing himself to be conned. He'd been infuriated with himself and Rozalia right up until discovering Trudi had been the real culprit.

Trudi's actions fit all his expectations of women, feeding his cynicism, but Rozalia's undisguised distress now rubbed a fresh and raw hole behind his breastbone.

She hadn't known he would never let her rot in jail. She must have been terrified.

"The earring was gone when I went downstairs," he said the minute they were enclosed in the back of his car. "I questioned my staff and asked the police to pay you a visit. Arresting you was overeagerness on their part. That wasn't my intention or request."

"No? I was sure it was more of your charming afterplay." Her voice was knife sharp and hard as steel. She took out her phone and made it clear she wished him under the wheels of his own car as it pulled away from the curb.

He took odd consolation from her deeply reviling remark. She might look worse for wear, but the woman inside was far from broken. He admired that spirit. Celebrated it.

"I'm leaving for the airport right now," he heard a woman say as Rozalia's first call was answered.

Glancing at the image, which he could only see at an angle, he imagined this was the cousin she had talked about so frequently. To say Gisella looked familiar to him would be an overstatement, but there was something in her even, feminine voice that sounded not unlike his mother's. There was also a resemblance in her high cheekbones and patrician brow.

"I'm out. It's okay. You don't have to come," Rozalia told her.

Gisella asked if she was coming home, then offered to come anyway, to wait with Rozalia until the lawyers closed the file.

"I'm not sure how long it will take. Can we talk later? I have to call Mom," Rozalia said.

"Yes, of course, but Rozi— Forget the earring, okay? It's not worth this kind of trouble."

Rozi. He liked that.

"Will you talk to Grandmamma about it?" She flicked him a glance of consternation. "I don't think we have the full story." Her phone buzzed midcall. "Oh, there's Mom, trying to reach me again. I need to go. I love you!"

The next call was full of tears on the American side of the screen, and many reassurances from Rozalia that she was fine. She was sorry she had caused a fuss. It was a misunderstanding. He lost track of the many ways she downplayed the situation.

"Why are you even still looking for those silly earrings?" her mother asked. "I thought you two had grown out of that."

"My phone is dying, Mom. I'll call you later, after I've had a shower and slept."

She clicked off her phone and dropped it into her purse,

then took stock as she realized they were arriving at a private airfield. Her eyes were red with emotion and now sharpened with accusation.

"I thought you were putting me on a bus."

"A bus," he repeated. "I do enjoy your sense of humor, Rozi. I've never been on a bus in my life."

The car stopped next to his helicopter and he escorted her into it.

CHAPTER FIVE

HE FLEW THE chopper with a copilot, which left her with no opportunity to talk to him, but that suited her fine. Was she supposed to thank him for getting her out of jail when he'd put her there?

Arresting you was overeagerness on their part.

Maybe, but he could have called *her* first thing this morning, rather than involving the police. Of course, if she had been some sort of international jewel thief, as he seemed to suspect, a phone call inquiring about the earring would have been her cue to get herself out of Dodge.

But she didn't want to see his side of it. She wanted to stay affronted and acrimonious because even if her arrest had been a misunderstanding, the way he had accused her of trying to trade her virginity for that earring was still insulting and hurtful.

She brooded the entire flight, only becoming aware of her surroundings as she saw the fading light hitting the Carpathian Mountains as they grew larger before them.

He landed behind a beautiful chalet tucked on a small plateau on the side of a valley.

"Your luggage was retrieved from the hotel. I'll bring it inside," he said as he helped her down to the lawn. "If the housekeeper is here, she'll unpack it for you."

She shrugged that off, capable of handling her own luggage and not wanting to talk to anyone right now. Instead of following him into the kitchen, she went up the steps at the side of the house to a veranda that circled around to jut out over the canyon. On one side, the view went up the valley to a lake puddled in a forest-rimmed plateau. The water was turning navy while the sky above it was stained pink and mauve. The water overflowed in a dozen small trickles that cascaded off the cliff in slivers of silver lace down a wall of greenery into the boulder-strewn river below.

In the other direction, the river widened and calmed as it meandered into foothills. A quaint village in the distance was a jumble of stone buildings and red tile roofs around the steeple of a church.

As she stood drinking in the sheer majesty of the world before her, she heard the whine and patter of the helicopter starting up. A moment later, it rose behind the house and faded back the way they'd come.

He hadn't even said goodbye. She swallowed, wondering why she was so bereft when this was exactly what she wanted—privacy to deal with all she'd been through since meeting him yesterday afternoon. She ought to breathe the biggest sigh of relief, but her chest ached. She hadn't expected he would disappear without saying another word to her, like he was discarding garbage at the landfill.

The door into the house clicked and Viktor came out to join her.

She jolted with surprise.

"I thought you left!" Panic returned in a rush as she strained and couldn't hear the helicopter at all. Leaving without saying anything would have been rude, but, "You're not staying here, are you?"

"Of course. The housekeeper stocked the kitchen and

left some food we can warm later. If we need anything, she can bring it when she comes back in a few days."

A few *days*?

She looked to the distant roofs of the village, wondering how long it would take her to walk there, in the dark. They must have a hotel of sorts, but would they have a room? Was there a taxi service in such a small town?

How much room was left on her credit card and how much would she need to get herself back to Budapest for her flight home?

"You told your mother you wanted to shower and sleep," Viktor reminded. "Shall I show you your room?"

She wanted that so badly, she nodded dumbly, abandoning the idea of leaving.

Maybe if the house hadn't been so exquisitely perfect, she might have clung to independence. Anxiety and weariness overwhelmed her, though, and she instinctively relaxed as she entered the interior of the house.

It was a very modern home and a feat of clever architecture, providing stunning views of the dusk-cloaked landscape from every window while leaving the impression it hung in midair on the side of the canyon. A few of the family's cherished antiques and priceless art pieces had made their way here, putting a classic stamp on the decor, but the high ceilings and earthy tones made it very much a retreat.

She was a city girl who walked through Central Park or went to the seaside to get back to nature. This forested vista was postcard beautiful and the kind of five-star surroundings she only experienced if her cousin spoiled her with a spa day.

"Is this your mother's room?" she asked as he brought her to a decidedly feminine bedroom with a luxurious en suite.

"She decorated this house over the tablet. I'm the only one who comes here. But the house was designed with the expectation I would bring a wife and family here one day. I use the adjoining room." He pointed to a pair of doors that would remain closed and locked, if she had anything to do with it.

"You think your future wife is going to appreciate you letting—" What should she call herself? Not his lover. His affair? His one-night stand? "—some other woman use this room before her?"

"We'll see, won't we?"

"*We* won't."

He didn't reply to that, only asked impassively, "Are you hungry?"

"Tired." It wasn't a lie. Mostly she needed time to regroup. He was too disturbing with his air of containment while being so watchful. She felt both judged and pitied. She didn't know if she was supposed to be angry or obliged.

Most of all, she kept thinking about the last time they'd been in a bedroom, naked and—

"I'd like a bath and to charge my phone. Is there Wi-Fi?"

He gave her the code and she locked herself into her room—not missing the irony of longing to get out of jail only to cage herself here, but this was voluntary and she needed time to think.

She tried to relax in the bath but went to bed with her mind still a whirl of confusion. It took her a long time to fall asleep. When she did, she slept until noon the following day. Some of her exhaustion was leftover jet lag and the aftermath of her horrendous experience in jail. A lot of it was a pity party. Every time she woke and remembered where she was, she decided she wasn't ready to face whatever was beyond those doors. Wasn't ready to speak to Viktor again. She rolled over and went back to sleep.

At one point she spent an hour answering texts from family, assuring everyone she was fine, but she was worried about Gisella. It sounded like she was seeing a lot of Kaine and was beholden to him because of her arrest. Rozi threw her arm over her eyes, wishing she hadn't put Gisella in that position, and silently promised her cousin she would fix it as soon as she got herself home.

Then she sought the blackout of sleep again.

When her stomach threatened to hunt down and kill something, she rose to fill it. She dressed in her yoga tights and a long T-shirt, then crept down the stairs. In the kitchen, a single plate was in the sink with a knife and fork.

The coffee pot was off, but the dregs in the carafe were still tepid. When she peeked back out to the lounge, she noticed a door off it, not closed completely. She could hear Viktor speaking Italian.

She put the dirty dishes in the dishwasher, then stood at the window. The mist off the waterfalls was casting rainbows against the granite wall behind them.

Damn this man's world and its spellbinding magic.

She started fresh coffee, then searched the fridge and cupboards, deciding to make *palacsinta* since the ingredients were here. The crepes were a comfort food for her and she really needed a taste of home right now.

Viktor entered as she was setting the small table in the kitchen nook. Had she thought twice about making enough for him? Absolutely. But she was not above taking the high ground out of spite, to prove she was better than someone she was mad at.

She just wished she could keep a firm grasp on her malevolence. Instead, she found herself feeling defensive, reacting to the sight of him, heart turning over while a shy smile of greeting tried to form on her lips. The ambivalence caused a physical ache behind her breastbone.

He wore dark pants with a cuff and a button shirt open at the throat. He'd shaved this morning and the spice of his aftershave was still faintly evident. His eyes held dark circles and his mouth was tense and unsmiling. He carried in an empty coffee mug and a plate with a few toast crumbs on it.

"Jó reggelt," he said, even though it was pushing midafternoon.

His voice caused a shiver of chill bumps all over her body.

"Good morning," she replied, pouring fresh coffee for him with an unsteady hand, then freshening her own.

"Thank you," he said.

She could feel the heat off his body and the crackle of dynamic energy he stored beneath that taut skin of his.

He was a powerful man. There was no denying it. Right or wrong, it was the way the world worked that the police would leap to do his bidding and suspect the outsider, the young woman with less money and an unknown reputation. If she *had* stolen the earring, arresting her would have been exactly what ought to have happened.

In fact, given that she had come all the way here to see the earring, it wasn't a stretch of anyone's imagination that she would be the first suspect when it went missing.

"Where was the earring?" She carried the plates of crepes, one savory, one sweet, to the table.

His mouth tightened as though he had to take firm control of his temper. "It was moved."

"By someone on your staff?"

"By a woman my mother wishes for me to marry."

"You're engaged?" She nearly dropped the plates.

"Not even close. Eat. You have to be hungry." He held a chair for her.

She had been snacking on fruit the entire time she'd been cooking, but lowered into the chair, freezing as a horrific thought occurred.

"When was she there?" she asked with appalled dread. "She wasn't downstairs when—"

"No," he cut in flatly. "She came by after you'd left. Endre didn't realize you'd gone so he didn't disturb me. He sent her away as quickly as he could."

"Oh." She had arranged a pretty array of fresh fruit and helped herself to it along with yogurt and muesli. "You didn't invite her, then."

"My mother had, without telling me." He sat and took a serving of the crepes. "She has encouraged Trudi to believe she is in contention for becoming my wife. Trudi saw a paparazzi photo of our arrival at the house. She was dismayed I had brought home a dinner guest when she thought *she* had a date with me."

"It's *her* fault I wound up in a cell? Moving the earring was a deliberate effort to have me blamed?"

"She claims it was for safekeeping, but you have a right to your outrage."

Rozi couldn't take that in. What sort of person *did* that?

"Your ring obviously means a lot to you. Did you make it?"

She sensed he was trying to change the subject to something less contentious. She glanced at the ring she rarely removed. "Gisella did."

"May I?" he held out his hand.

She tentatively offered hers, bracing herself for the *zing* as he gently clasped her fingers and studied the rose gold setting of vine leaves around the rainbow mosaic inside a black opal. Small diamonds glistened as dewdrops against the leaves, giving the ring some sparkle, but Rozalia wasn't someone who flaunted and flashed. Gisella knew that. It was fairly understated unless you took the time to study it.

Viktor used his thumb to move the ring incrementally, watching the shift of colors inside the stone.

"Half the time people think it's a mood ring, which suits me. Otherwise I might get mugged," she joked, trying not to react to his innocuous touch, but her nerve endings were jittering. "It's actually quite a rare stone. Blues and greens are common and flecks of red aren't unusual, but this one has pinks and yellows. Even glints of gold."

"It's an opal?"

"The least practical gem," she agreed with a rueful twitch of her mouth. "They can crack, but Gizi knows I adore them. The way it's cut and set should protect it from all but deliberate mistreatment, though."

"It's more than meets the eye on first glance." His gaze lifted to hers and something in his tone made her heart stutter. "Was it a birthday present?"

"A graduation gift." She withdrew her hand and nervously picked up her fork, accidentally clanking it against the edge of her plate. "We're the same age and do almost everything together. School, apprenticeship... Our uncle commissioned us to make a ring for each other and left it to us to judge whether we had mastered our vocation."

Viktor's brows went up with interest. He reached for his cutlery while keeping his attention firmly on her, encouraging her to expand on that.

"Making jewelry on spec is one thing and you'll almost always find a buyer for your vision if you wait long enough, but if you want to make a living, you have to be able to set aside your own preferences and give the customer what appeals to them. This isn't anything like what Gisella would make for herself." Rozi rotated her wrist.

"She made what she knew I would love and I do. So I said she was ready."

"What did you make for her?"

She glanced for her phone, wishing she could protest that she'd left it upstairs, but it was right there where his long arm easily snagged it off the end of the counter.

She flicked to pull up the art deco ring of tapered baguettes in a rainbow of seven colors and handed it to him. "I wanted it to represent our generation of cousins. Gisella sometimes feels she's not really one of us, since her grandfather was Istvan, not Benedek."

"So she always has the strength of her family with her," he mused, studying the photo.

Her heart took another trip, startled that he grasped her intention so quickly. "Yes." She strained to swallow.

"It's beautiful." He handed back the phone, gaze on her again. Not on her ring, or her chest, *her*. As if he was seeing facets he hadn't seen before.

She went back to eating, wishing it was as easy to hide herself as it was to tuck her ring hand under the table and into her lap.

"I'm worried about her," she murmured, more to deflect from herself than anything else. "I don't know why she turned to Kaine Michaels to pay for my legal fees."

"I'll take care of that bill."

"That's not what I was driving at. I was just…" Making conversation. She set down her fork and tucked both hands in her lap, so he couldn't see how she was nervously twisting her ring. He completely disarmed her.

All she could think about was their intensely intimate night. She'd been wrung with an intense pleasure that had been a type of agony. Now she was in agony again, but it was one she embraced, because being in his presence was both torture and joy. She ought to know when to cut her losses, and not sit here longing to find their way out of the hurt and misunderstandings to a place with potential. There wasn't such a thing. Not for them. And she hadn't stayed with him the other night expecting long-term. She had known it was a one-off. That's why—

"Oh, my God!" She covered her mouth with both hands, recollection striking like an anvil smashing a piano, filling her ears with a discordant crash.

"What?" he demanded, looking around, instantly going on high alert at her clear alarm.

She could feel the blood draining out of her face, a shock even greater than getting arrested flowing over her like an ice bath. If she hadn't been sitting, she would have fallen down. As it was, she had to take hold of the table to maintain her balance in the chair.

"Rozi," he urged, grasping her wrist as she uncovered her mouth. "Tell me."

"It was too late when I got back to my hotel," she said faintly, mortified and horrified. *Scared.* "I meant to go in the morning, but the police came. I was arrested, then we came here." She spoke faster as she saw his expression closing up with tense suspicion.

He let go her arm and sat back, expression carved from granite.

"I forgot, Viktor. I honestly *forgot.*"

Was he surprised? Not at all.

He sat very still, allowing this information to filter like a cool breeze through the events of the last two and a half days. She had upended his equilibrium from the moment she had appeared like a sprite out of thin air, chatting up his driver, then turning her charm on him, shoving her way into his car and teasing out his most deeply regressed memories.

"I didn't skip it on purpose. I'm not trying to trick you into marriage or support or something. You had me *arrested*."

"I did not want or direct that you be arrested. Believe that," he ordered, hackles rising. He was many things, but not someone who sent innocents to jail.

She snorted, gaze trying to reflect pithy disdain, but there was a lingering shadow of injury beneath.

Even so, he held her stare with a hard one of his own, daring her to accuse him one more time of putting her in a cell. She looked away first, flinching.

"Your girlfriend did, then," she allowed in a low voice. "Either way, I would have taken the pill if the arrest hadn't happened. I intended to. I *wanted* to." She was wringing her hands beneath the edge of the table again.

Whether her seemingly tortured conscience was real or not didn't concern him, which was odd. This news certainly shouldn't be sending pulses of possibility shooting into his brain because, virginity notwithstanding, she wasn't as innocent as she appeared. Hell, he was still convinced their lovemaking had been an attempt to persuade him to give up the earring.

She hadn't pressed her right to it, though. She'd left in a whirl of scorn the other night, which he had seen as another screen of deceit once he discovered the earring was missing.

Finding it gone hadn't surprised him one iota. Nevertheless, even as he'd been snapping out terse orders to call the police and question the staff, something in him had grasped with satisfaction at having an excuse to see her again.

Then he'd learned she hadn't taken the earring. *That* had surprised him. He had gladly eschewed his tightly scheduled meetings and other deadlines to free her from a cell and fly her here. He had installed her in his personal refuge, seizing the chance to spend more time with her, wanting to get to the bottom of exactly what kind of woman she was.

She had ignored him all night, worrying him a little, she had slept so long, but he'd caught up on some of the work he'd shirked. He'd also spent a good portion of the evening brooding on her hurt as she had stormed out the other night. On the blame and anguish she'd expressed at being arrested.

He had almost convinced himself he had misjudged her. As he sat here, eating delicious food that she had prepared for him, he had been trying to find words to apologize for Trudi's behavior.

Now this.

But where was the alarm he ought to feel at what had to be a premeditated, underhanded plan? Where was his outrage?

It was eclipsed by a Neanderthal response that reveled in the idea of his seed taking root in her, binding her to him. He barely knew her and certainly didn't trust her, but barbarism rose as a possessive force inside him, still drunk on their erotic experience and longing to repeat it. He had to push past the blind haze and force his mind to the civilized, rational reaction.

"If you're pregnant with my baby, would you keep it?"

Flashes of emotion sparked out of her expression in the myriad shades of her opal—shock that he had asked such a forthright question, daunted fear, fault and culpability along with something more helpless, then a more contemplative look that softened to tender yearning.

That vulnerable array of feelings shouldn't captivate him, but it did. It shook the reinforced walls inside him, leaving veins of hairline fractures.

"I would want *my* child, yes." Her words rang with emotion, seeming to come straight from her heart.

He smiled faintly, distantly aware of his own heart pounding like a sledgehammer in heavy thwacks behind his breastbone. "But mine?"

"I don't understand what you're asking. This isn't arbitrary. It's not like I don't care who I make a baby with."

"No, of course not." He reached for his coffee.

"Are you suggesting I would only want your baby because you're wealthy? That I slept with you intending this?"

"Why else?" He kept having flashes of that moment when he'd first thrust into her, the way she had clamped so tightly to him, her gasp of distress turning to a dreamy sigh that had inspired profound protectiveness in him. Deep, misguided possessiveness still gripped him even as he was convinced she was entrapping him.

Her mouth opened in soundless outrage.

"I was carried away by passion. Something I'd never felt before." She searched his expression as if looking for an echo of the same thing in him.

He quickly closed himself against revealing how exceptional the experience had been for him. Sexual intimacy should never be confused as something more profound. *He knew that.*

As he kept his thoughts and feelings hidden behind a stoic mask, her expression faded into anxiety of exposure and a flinch of hurt that made his heart lurch.

"Why did *you* sleep with *me*?" she challenged with an angry hair flip, glints of agony still evident behind her eyes. "I was handy and willing? At least I was attracted to you. Was," she repeated flatly, rising and snatching up her dishes.

Her insult was pure face saving and his ego was not that

fragile, but he was compelled to catch at her wrist, not letting her swing away with her handful of plates.

"You were mindless with pleasure? That's what you want me to believe?"

He found himself *wanting* to believe it.

Her mouth trembled with persecution before she brought her chin up in defiance.

"You were the experienced one and didn't put on a condom. Go ahead and act like I'm some coldhearted hustler, but that makes you a dupe. Is that what you are?"

That one did land with a sting. He had been a sucker once and vowed never to let it happen to him again.

He found himself rising reflexively to grasp her tense jaw in a finger and thumb, splaying his fingertips against the soft flesh in her throat where her pulse throbbed.

"Pure passion? That's what you want me to believe? Let's test that, shall we?"

Her pupils dilated.

He might have thought it fear, but she made no move to step away or brush him off. She stood in his light hold as if transfixed by his touch. He could practically taste the pheromones rising off her skin, interacting with his own primal signals, eroding his control.

He gave in to the draw and covered her mouth with his, inundated at the first touch with earthy, poetic sensations of crushed rose petals, mountain air and the unique, hot flavor in the caverns of her mouth.

He moved closer, caressed the back of her neck to encourage her to arch into him while his other hand found her breast. Her nipple beaded hard enough to thrust against his palm through her bra and shirt. He massaged lazily, swallowing her shaken sigh, while the haze of lust encroached further, urging him to have her again. Fully. *Now.*

She started to twine an arm around his neck, dropping

the dishes as she did. One clipped his elbow before they both landed with a shatter. Pieces of crockery hit his leg.

Rozi gasped and leaped back.

He was in rubber-soled slippers. She was barefoot. He quickly caught her up to keep her from stepping on any of the jagged edges and pivoted to sit her on the end of the counter. Snatching up a paper towel, he wiped the jam off her foot and ensured both were uninjured.

"I'm fine," she said, curling her toes against his grip on her arches, picking her feet out of his grip and trying to slide to the floor again.

He set a hand on her thigh. "Stay there," he ordered, then found the broom and dustpan to gather the mess.

"I slept with you because I was reckless and impulsive and stupid," she said from her perch. "But I won't make it worse by doing it again."

Her voice lost a lot of power as he flashed her a glance, blood still hot with lust. The receptive flick of her tongue against his and the pebbled nipple against his palm were still imprinted on his flesh.

"No?"

Rozi couldn't hold his gaze. She cleared her throat and her palms hurt where she gripped the lip of marble she sat upon.

"I wasn't *trying* to make your baby. I'll walk to the village as soon as we're finished playing 'the floor is lava' and get the pill."

"It's called the morning after pill because you're supposed to take it the morning after. We're long past that," he said flatly. "You already told me what your decision would be if there turns out to be a baby."

"That doesn't mean I *want* to be…pregnant." She tried to take hold of the agitation thinning her voice. Tried not to panic. "I won't be accused of scheming to make this happen, Viktor. You're the one who—"

"I know what I've done." He cut her off with a tone that was so decisive and flat it made her sit very still, as though the first tremor of an earthquake had her unconsciously bracing for the bigger shakes to come. "*I* was reckless," he stated with self-castigation. "I know better than to take undue risks with my health and with…this."

He jerked his head to the ceiling, indicating his house on the hill that stood as a symbol of all that he was and oversaw.

"I won't shirk my responsibility again." He shook the mess off the dustpan into the wastebasket, then washed his hands.

Part of her wanted him to take the blame for this, but premonition of disaster went through her at his words. When he held out his hands so she could steady herself on his arms, she dropped to her feet. But even as her fingertips dug into his muscles, she understood there to be as much cage as support in these iron-hard arms.

She couldn't breathe and had to strain to speak.

"We were both reckless," she said. "This…" She flicked her fingertips at her middle. "Doesn't have to become your responsibility."

"Don't be naive, Rozi." The way he spoke her nickname was a disconcerting mix of the way her family lovingly shortened it and his own thickly accented, unique appropriation of the two syllables. It was comforting and familiar, yet sexy and gruff.

Disarming.

Or maybe it was simply that her emotions were growing heightened as she sensed her grip on her life slipping away and falling under his firm, ruthless control.

"I'm not naive. I'm from *New York*," she protested.

"I'm sure you're very worldly in many ways," he scoffed. "But even if we got you a pill before the end of today, we would still have to wait out the result. So let's wait."

"Are you out of your mind? Then I really might repeat my grandmother's life, raising a child alone in New York." She waved a hand in a direction that might be west. She was too disoriented to have any sense of space and time right now.

"You wouldn't go back to America," he said, voice so commanding, her ears rang. "If you're pregnant, you'll stay here. And marry me."

CHAPTER SIX

"MY LIFE IS in New York," Rozalia argued a short while later, after she finished tidying the kitchen and they moved into the lounge. "My flight home is Friday. My uncle expects me back at work Monday."

"You'll have to change those arrangements, stay here until we know. When would you normally expect…" He glanced at her abdomen.

"My 'woman's time'?" she provided facetiously. Why were men so flummoxed by something that was so normal? "In about…" She cleared her throat and folded her arms defensively, remorseful as she admitted, "Ten or twelve days."

As timing went, they had taken a risk at precisely the optimal time to conceive.

That's probably why she'd slept with him. Her ovaries had been bursting with fertility. One whiff of his high-grade testosterone and her inner cavewoman had taken control of her senses, throwing her into bed with him.

She could still feel his muscled thighs pushing hers apart, his weight and heat and burning kisses. She had felt so elemental and raw, yet safe. That had been the startling part—that she had been profoundly vulnerable, but not frightened or alone. He had been with her, holding her, joining her as the very power of life had overtaken them.

She had believed he was glorying in that wondrous place *with* her. A place where they expressed themselves with their whole bodies, arching and feeling, bonding and shattering in unison.

Her lack of experience had obviously elevated the experience into more than it was. She was still behaving like a callow virgin because she was still reacting to him. Their kiss in the kitchen had had her forgetting that she held plates. Now, to her mortification, thinking of their lovemaking caused perspiration to break out on her upper lip. It took everything she had to disguise that her body was readying for him all over again, heating from the middle out with sweet, receptive tingles.

"Convenient," he said, making her grossly self-conscious until she realized he was doing the math on their timing.

"Exactly the reason I don't want to 'wait and see.'" She flicked a hand at his thinly veiled accusation. "I was a virgin. I was arrested. You brought me here where I have no options, but you keep accusing me of being the one playing the oldest trick in the book. I don't want to be tied to someone who thinks that's what kind of person I am."

He made an impatient noise and clicked on a lamp against a gloom that gathered as clouds thickened beyond the windows.

"I don't want to believe I was weak-headed enough to let you take advantage of me, but your motives don't matter. I made an error in judgment by having unprotected sex. I can't turn my back on the potential consequences of that. So you stay here with me until we know where we stand."

"You're really prepared to marry someone you don't trust?"

"I don't trust anyone. Don't take it personally."

"Okay. How about someone you barely *respect*?"

"I hold you in higher regard than Trudi," he said with a curl of his lip.

"There's a high bar. I'm flattered," she dismissed scathingly.

"What do you *want*, Rozalia?" He sounded as though he was barely holding on to his patience. "I'm willing to do the honorable thing. I don't understand why you're upset about it."

"Because I don't want to face what my grandmother faced! That's why I was still a virgin, okay? Because my cousin and I agreed we wouldn't sleep with anyone until we were sure we had a future with whoever it was." Until they believed they were *in love*.

"I've said we'll marry."

"That's not a future!"

"How is it not? It sounds as though you grew up on a shoestring. This would be a very advantageous marriage for you." He sounded insulted.

"And that is why we don't have a future! You think I'm here to better myself and I'm *not*. What did I do to make you think I'm so driven by self-interest?"

"Aside from the possible pregnancy?"

She threw up a hand in vexation and looked to the door.

"*Everyone* is driven by self-interest," he said, quiet and harsh. "Every acquaintance asks for a professional favor. The most devoted and trusted employees are motivated by a generous salary, nothing else. Even my own mother expects me to elevate her social position with my marriage. It doesn't make sense that you gave up your virginity for an orgasm."

"I happen to think that's a best-case scenario for anyone's first time," she shot back. "What did you want from *me*? Sexier moves? A color TV? What's the real issue here,

Viktor? That you think I brought more to our transaction and you don't know how to square it off?"

His cheek ticked.

"Oh, my God." She faltered. "That's it, isn't it? Listen, I gave you my virginity because I wanted to. Enjoy that gift. There are no shoestrings attached. But understand that I've spent most of my life getting to where I am professionally. Taking my place in the back of the family shop is all I ever wanted. My *family* is far too important to me to risk on purpose. Of course I would stay here and raise my baby with its father if that happened. Of course I would. But do you think I *want* to lose what I have? That I want to raise my baby away from my m-mom?"

The sheer magnitude of what they were discussing struck her. She bit her lips and looked to the window, aware that her entire life hung, like this house, off the edge of a cliff. She blinked a sudden sting from her eyes. Her voice turned into a thick scrape in the back of her throat.

"I'm not standing here dreaming of how to spend your money, Viktor. I'm terrified I've blown up my life in a way I can't fix."

She was starting to feel as trapped as she had been in that holding cell. Behind the throb in her breastbone, her heart was palpitating as she mentally searched for the path back to her life in America. To the safe arms of people who loved her.

Into the harrowing silence, his phone buzzed. He glanced at it. "My mother. I need to speak to her." He lifted his head to rake her with his gaze. "I'll take my call, you make yours."

To change her travel arrangements, he meant.

He disappeared into his study before she could say anything more.

* * *

Viktor endured a contentious conversation with his mother. She was "deeply concerned" that he was spending time with the American girl who had caused unseemly press coverage, attaching an investigation by the police to the family name.

Viktor pointed out that Trudi's machinations had been the reason the police had entered their hallowed gates. "If you would prefer I make that public, Mother, I will."

She hadn't been ready to back down, arguing against him entertaining Rozalia at his chalet. "If Trudi isn't right for you, there is a lovely young woman—"

"I no longer require your services in finding me a bride," he stated, firmly curtailing any future efforts.

"You're not going to marry this girl!" she protested with alarm. "I looked up the family when they contacted me. Her cousin, yes. I could live with that if she wasn't your cousin. But this one? *No.* They're plebeians."

He didn't mention the possibility that the next Rohan heir was taking root in Rozi's womb right now. He knew what his mother would say to that—that he had walked into a baited trap.

Had he? He couldn't get the vision of Rozi's stark profile out of his mind's eye. The way her mouth had trembled as she contemplated raising her child away from her family. He'd had an enormous compulsion to hug her in comfort, which had flummoxed him. He enjoyed physical contact in bed, but he wasn't an affectionate or demonstrative man.

"If and when I decide to marry, Mother, you'll be the first to know." He then asked after his aunt and was still tense when he hung up, thinking about Rozi's distress.

He was caught between trusting what he'd learned years ago—that no one could be trusted—and believing a more gut-level instinct that told him Rozi was exactly what she said she was—a young woman who had succumbed to desire.

That shouldn't be impossible to believe. *He* had.

And the desire to succumb again and again consumed him.

That pit of unending hunger drove him more urgently than any other force. Did he want a wife and child? He had always expected he would have at least one of each, but it wasn't something he'd felt a strong desire to acquire. Did he want the baby that Rozi might carry? He could state firmly, yes. He did. But it was very much a philosophical want.

What he wanted in a more visceral, concrete way was Rozi. And if the price of that was marriage, he found himself ridiculously ready to pay it.

While she seemed genuinely apprehensive that she might have to marry him. Even the most cynical pockets of his mind couldn't dismiss that her life would change a lot more than his own if they married and started a family. It was sobering to recognize that. Enough that he grew concerned when he left his office and couldn't find her.

Her things were still in her room, the door open, so she hadn't gone far.

He went through the rest of the house, glanced out to see the car was in the garage. As often happened in the mountains, the weather had completely changed. Heavy rain had begun falling. If she had decided to walk, she would get soaked. Or lost.

He was about to shrug on a weatherproof jacket and go looking for her when he realized she had been curled into the wicker love seat on the covered veranda.

She rose and came into the house with her sketchbook under her arm, an empty teacup in her hand. The absorbed expression on her delicate features altered as she realized he was standing there, waiting for her.

If she was a con artist, she was beyond excellent at portraying purity of heart, managing a faint blush that was utterly fascinating before she dropped her lashes and self-consciously pressed her lips together.

"It's getting cold."

The far side of the canyon had all but disappeared as the storm continued to gather in shrouds of heavy mist against the rocky walls.

"Were you making calls?" He was used to getting the result he wanted with a command and needed—yes, *needed*—to know she wasn't leaving on Friday.

"I don't know what to say to them," she said with a perplexed shrug.

"Tell them we're involved and you're staying to see where it goes." It wasn't untrue.

"We're *waiting.* Not *dating.*"

"We're doing both. My mother has bowed out of an appearance in Venice. We'll leave in the morning and attend in her place."

"I can't leave the country."

"Commercial airlines may give you grief. You'll be with me. You'll be fine."

"I'm not really the spotlight type, Viktor. And wouldn't that just start rumors about us?" She shook her head in rejection.

"I'm pleased to start new rumors. My mother has been encouraging speculation about Trudi. I won't have her associated with our family any longer." *That* was nonnegotiable and he'd made sure his mother understood it.

"So call one of your other girlfriends."

"Why are you pushing back like this? We need to get ahead of the story. If you're pregnant, we want it to seem deliberate and within the confines of a committed relationship. You are not interchangeable with any other woman."

The truth in that statement rang through him like the peal of a bell, the vibration striking so deeply it was uncomfortable. "It will be nothing more strenuous than smiling graciously while a politician praises the artwork we are repatriating. You like art." He indicated the sketchbook she held.

She hugged it tighter to her middle as though he had tried to take it.

He lifted a brow, surprised. "Are your designs proprietary? Do *you* not trust *me*?" Why did *that* thought bother him?

She snorted in a way that suggested the jury was definitely still out. "No matter how quickly you might steal my brilliant ideas and knock out your own versions, the developing-world costume manufacturers are way ahead of you. You must have issues with piracy yourself?"

"We do." But patent infringements affecting his factories were far down his list of priorities at the moment. "Why the defensiveness, then?" He nodded at the book. "Are you sensitive to criticism? I understand many artists are. I'll be gentle."

"I'm not that thin-skinned," she muttered, handing over the book and moving to set aside her empty mug. "I often ask Gizi or my uncle for an opinion on my designs before I start the real work. But most of the drawings in that book aren't meant for anyone's eyes but mine. I sketch when I need to think."

"A type of journaling?" If so, her mind was a garden of mood and introspection. Both soothing and intriguing. A nice place to get lost.

He had almost hoped for math calculations on how she would budget out a paternity settlement. Fuel for mistrust would be easier to take than the way she was upending his view of how the world worked.

He scanned through simple, yet compelling mushrooms and cityscapes. Some sketches were complete, others showed the barest suggestion of an object. Pigeons, a mandala and a bicycle wheel were interspersed between eye-catching broaches and pendants, earrings and bracelets. Nature and need. Hard and soft. Contrasts and complements. Nothing was one simple thing.

The final pages were the uprights in his veranda, an ethereal impression of the mist-obscured lake, and his own profile rendered in a series of spare, austere lines that made something shift inside him.

He had wanted a window into her mind, but somehow she had stripped him bare with a few pencil strokes. The entire book was worth a longer study, but he grew almost as uncomfortable viewing his image as she had seemed before she had allowed him to see it.

He handed the book back to her, not knowing what to say except, "You're very good."

"It's just doodling," she dismissed. "And it didn't help. No matter what I say, my mother won't understand how I could even consider a romantic relationship with someone so far away. I briefly dated a man whose family lived in Boston and she was beside herself that I would move there."

Boston? That man could go to hell, he thought reflexively, then wondered where such instant antipathy had come from.

"How was your conversation with your mother? How is your aunt?"

"Turned her ankle in the garden. Not nearly as serious as feared. A sprain and a few bruises."

"It sounds like she's very active. I think she's around my grandmother's age? Grandmamma celebrated her eightieth birthday two years ago."

"Bella Néni is eighty-one and, yes, very spry. She has some live-in staff, but age hasn't slowed her down. She's as self-sufficient as I am." He dryly referenced the fact he probably had more staff cooking and cleaning for him than his elderly aunt employed.

"Could I meet her?"

"Why?"

"Because I came to Hungary to learn more about our family history. I'd like to talk to your mother, too, if she's willing. Especially now that you've accused my grandmother of *stealing* the earrings. That definitely needs clearing up."

This was leverage, he recognized, but felt churlish using it. At the same time, he was only growing more determined to continue the course he had set.

"Change your travel arrangements and come to Venice. I'll take you to see Aunt Bella as soon after that as our schedule allows."

CHAPTER SEVEN

WHAT WAS MOTHER NATURE trying to tell her? Rozi wondered, when she found herself on the veranda of the chalet watching lightning fork around her. Thunder boomed and she hunched a little deeper into the blanket she pinched closed around herself, but stayed where she was.

She was a *very* idealistic person. She wanted to believe things worked out for the best, that there were depths of goodness in everyone around her. She had to believe that, otherwise she wouldn't be able to face the cruelty and darkness in this harsh, ruthless world.

She was also fanciful enough to believe the universe was putting all these roadblocks in her way because she was meant to stay here with Viktor, even though he was the furthest thing from the future she had imagined for herself. She had always expected to marry for love. She wanted children, and in her vision, she had a big, tumbling family like the one she came from.

Of course, hers would have one key difference. *Her* husband would be a man of means, not that she faulted her father. He was idealistic and she loved him all the more for his generous heart, but she wanted a husband who made a point of paying the electric bill on time.

She had *not* aspired to a husband as rich as Viktor. And

his level of means was hardly compensation for what she really, really wanted in her marriage.

Her dream of marrying for love would have to be abandoned if she was pregnant with his child. She was struggling to accept that. In fact, her family's streak of optimism was strong enough in her that she kept wondering if they were *meant* to repeat and revise Istvan and Eszti's story, this time with a happier ending?

Would he come to love her? Eventually?

Fool, the skies blasted in a flash of lightning, then blackened and growled a warning against being so delusional.

Viktor wasn't a bad man, but he wasn't one with an open heart. They'd had a night of passion and he'd shown her nothing but suspicion since. She couldn't marry that.

But what other option did she have if she was pregnant?

What if she wasn't pregnant and went home and never saw him again?

"You like it out here."

She jumped at the sound of his voice, dragged from her deep ruminations back to the steady patter of rain that had muffled the sound of the door.

He came to stand beside her and a frisson of awareness, like the ions that attracted lightning, gathered around her.

At least I would have that, she thought. Passion wasn't love, though. And one-sided passion wouldn't sustain a marriage. Her small ray of hope disappeared with the dim light as he clicked off the flashlight he held and the world went pitch-black.

"The power went out?" she guessed.

"Yes." He'd been working in his study and that was likely the only reason he'd abandoned his precious laptop to find her.

Another flash and boom resounded, one on top of the other. It was so loud she squeaked and instinctively hunched closer to him in the dark.

"We're fine," he said calmly and drew her in to his side with a heavy arm. "It was over there."

"I can't see where you're pointing."

"Across the valley." His voice was a quiet growl, strangely soothing. She felt an impulse to slip her arm around his waist, but she was trapped inside the cocoon of her blanket and his arm around her.

Still, she felt safe enough to ask, "Do you believe in destiny?"

"I do not." His tone was gentle, but final. "I believe in opportunity. Pay attention when it arises because it may not come around again."

A gust of spitting rain swept across them, dampening her face while a rumble sounded in the distance.

"I don't want to think of my child as an *opportunity*." Beneath the wrap of the blanket, she shifted her hand to cover her abdomen. "I have always wanted my children to be the result of love. Isn't that what you would want?"

She needed to know he had the capacity to love, at the very least.

She felt him draw a breath and exhale it, as though readying himself to deliver unpleasant news.

"I thought once that I might marry for love. There was a young woman I had feelings for."

A slash of pain went through her, searing as a lightning strike, leaving a scorched sensation behind her heart. It was so sharp and surprising, she lost her breath and almost didn't hear the rest of what he said.

"She died in the car crash that killed my brother. That was how I learned they were involved. Her sister told me at the funeral that she preferred me, but the wiser choice was to marry the heir, so she began seeing Kristof behind my back."

"He went along with that?" How could his brother do that to him?

"At my mother's urging, yes."

Her ears rang at such treachery. She couldn't imagine anyone being so coldhearted toward anyone, especially their own family. No wonder he didn't believe in love and loyalty. No wonder he was so distrustful of her motives.

"I'm sorry, Viktor. That's awful." She tried to turn toward him, but his arm became iron hard around her, holding her in place, side by side.

She blinked and craned her neck, opened her eyes wide, but it was too dark to see his face. Perhaps that was why he was willing to share something so intimate.

"Why should you apologize?" He was speaking without emotion, but she could feel the undercurrents of betrayal still seething in him. "It has nothing to do with you. I'm simply explaining why I leap to the assumption everyone operates out of self-interest, no matter how highly you might regard them."

"You'll never see me as anything but mercenary," she realized, shrugging from his hold and snuggling the blanket more firmly around her, suddenly feeling the damp chill in the air. "I happen to be the complete opposite, you know. I believe you when you say you're trying to be honorable. But I'm not so blinded by the bright side that I don't recognize you have a lot more resources if you decide I'm not suitable as your wife and sue me for custody of our child."

"I wouldn't do that." He sounded insulted by the suggestion.

"And my naive optimism tells me to believe you. Who becomes the fool in *that* situation, though?"

The storm moved down the valley and lightning danced in the foothills, briefly outlining his silhouette while thunder rolled back toward them.

"Viktor, I appreciate that you want to do the right thing, but children should be wanted. This isn't something you want. I can tell." *She* wasn't something he wanted.

Another gust of wind threw a spatter of rain across her. The blanket was getting damp enough to be uncomfortable. So was this conversation. She tried to search out the door and he clicked on the flashlight to follow her in.

"It's true that, until this happened, children were one more assignment I was required to complete, something I would procure through an advantageous marriage." He moved to the fireplace. Kindling was already in place and it only took a single match to start small flames licking upward. They cast long shadows and a muted glow through the room.

"All part of expanding your empire?" How sad that sounded.

"Yes." He rose. "But my mother will be comfortable the rest of her days no matter what I do. My aunt is also very well-off. That means the decisions I make today are for me and my offspring."

He stared into the fire, expression unreadable.

"I don't wish the mother of my progeny to be an arbitrary choice," he said in a remote voice. "I have no desire—literally—to procreate with someone whose chief reason for being in my bed is because my mother has vetted her as financially and socially suitable. Mother's tastes do not match my own," he said, turning his head to reveal the shadows in his deadpan expression.

"Weird," she said facetiously. "But you still don't want *me*."

"Don't I?"

That tiny fire wasn't throwing the amount of heat that suffused her.

"I'm not talking about sex," she muttered, although she had some doubts on that front, too. He might want her in a clinical sense. He might grow aroused by the fact she was female, but it had nothing to do with *her*.

He set a bigger chunk of wood on the fire, then brushed his hand on his thigh.

"I'm talking about more than sex. My mother didn't care for childbearing. Or the rearing, for that matter. That was left to nannies. Since I arrived at adulthood, she and I have had what I would describe as a business relationship. My relationship with my father was much the same. His interest in my grades was more about my potential aptitude for the corporate world than pride in my accomplishments. He was a role model for work ethic and negotiation, not attentive in the least."

"And your brother?"

A pause, then, "I thought he was my best friend."

Until he had stolen Viktor's girlfriend on the way to his own funeral.

Her heart weighed heavier in her chest.

She moved a pair of chairs away from the dining room table and unwrapped the blanket from around herself, draping it across the backs to dry. Then she sat on the sofa.

"I wouldn't be like your parents," she said, clasping her hands and willing him to believe her. "My family is very close-knit. I can't imagine being anything but completely involved in my children's lives. That's why I'm so apprehensive about this. Once I'm in, I'm so far in I'll never get out. That's petrifying."

"I believe you would care about our child. That's why I'm letting this play out."

"But I want to build a fulfilling life with someone I love

who wants our children as much as I do. Not be the surrogate for your baby and double as its nanny!" She opened her helpless palms, pleading with him to understand.

His nostrils pinched as he drew a sharp breath, as though absorbing an unexpected blow. "I would endeavor to be a more involved father than I had, Rozalia."

His stiff expression in the low light struck her as defensive. Her stupid, sensitive, insensible heart wrenched inside her chest. He was a man of untold wealth, but she was the one with the richer life, she realized with sudden clarity.

And she was defeated by that. By the recognition that she was the one in possession of something he needed—a heart. Her upbringing wouldn't allow her to do anything but open hers to him. Offer it.

"Are the cell phones working?" she asked.

"The landline is."

"I'll call Mom."

Late the next afternoon, Viktor walked into the top-floor suite of a sixteenth-century palazzo overlooking the Grand Canal in Venice and knocked on the closed bedroom door.

"I'm back. Do you want a drink?" he called.

Rozi had been pensive as they traveled. He had retreated, as well, having shared more than he intended to last night. She had capitulated to extending her stay, however, and had come here without protest. She had even expressed interest in the painting he was donating, then declined the stylist he offered and chose a gown herself from the selection he'd had brought in.

All this so they could begin "dating." What a ridiculously pale word for the complex relationship they had formed on a very short acquaintance.

She swung open the door. "I can't have alcohol until I know," she reminded him.

"You're ready," he said, stunned as much by the fact she was dressed with shoes on as by her finished appearance.

He didn't have a particular fetish for women dressed to the nines. Cleavage and heels were always a view he appreciated, but he found the layers of couture gowns and pristine makeup and teased-up hairstyles to be a type of look-but-don't-touch armor. One that *always* took hours.

"I come from a family of six with one bathroom. I know how to get myself together in the time allotted."

Did she ever. Her mauve gown wasn't the most flamboyant choice, but it flattered her figure and allowed her inner fire to shine through. She had combed her hair into a waterfall of lush waves scooped off one ear, revealing a single gold hoop in her lobe. Her makeup enhanced her natural prettiness with earthy shades, and a nude shine on her lips was both sensual and kissable.

This wasn't the *objet d'art* he was used to escorting, but a living, breathing woman, warm and vibrant and compelling. The only thing holding him off from touching her was the wariness she was still exhibiting, moving nervously back into the bedroom to gather a few things into her clutch.

"You look lovely." He made himself go the other direction and pour a drink for himself, to steady his voice and control.

"Thank you." She faltered as she joined him in the lounge, frowning in confusion. "Don't we have to leave?"

"It's my habit to pad the departure time for my dates." He spritzed soda into orange juice for her. "You continue to surprise me."

Her brows went up in exaggerated indignation.

"At least there's time to exchange that if you don't like it." He nodded to the velvet box he'd fetched from the lobby.

"From downstairs?" she asked with the complete opposite of delight. A small cringe, in fact. "Please say it's a loan?"

That took him off guard. He was always generous and wasn't used to his gifts receiving anything but squeals of enthusiasm. "I bought it. They have an excellent reputation."

"You know you're paying for convenience in a place like this, right?" She sent him a look of exasperation. "Promise me that no matter what happens between you and I, you'll let our shop vet your purchases moving forward. Mmm." That was a sound of dismay as she peered at what was in the box.

"I told them we had an event and I wanted to make a statement." He wanted the world to know she had value to him and he wanted *her* to know it. Maybe he'd also thought the diamonds a suitable inducement, given her trepidation at staying with him, but, "I genuinely thought it would look lovely on you."

"Something this generic looks good on anyone. It looks good on a mannequin. But it's designed to move stones, not hearts." She pulled her loupe from her clutch and bent her head.

"You carry that with you?"

"Cell phone, credit card, loupe, lip balm, bus pass," she listed off her essentials on her fingers and thumb. "The cut and clarity are nice. Even so, they can do better. And should." She lifted her head. "Can I talk to them?"

"Are you going to make a scene?" He took a hit off the scotch he'd poured for himself, truly confounded by her reaction.

"I'm always very nice when I dress someone down." She blinked her lengthened lashes. "You barely felt it at all."

* * *

Rozalia emerged from the manager's office twenty minutes later, thankful to be wearing a tasteful and truly interesting necklace of amethysts set in platinum.

Was Viktor annoyed with her? Insulted that she had rejected his gift? She couldn't tell. He lifted his head from reading his phone to peruse her new adornment, then met her anxious gaze with a completely impassive expression.

"I agree," he stated dryly.

Was he patronizing her?

The manager fell over himself apologizing to Viktor, crediting him with a full refund for the original necklace and not charging for the one Rozi now wore.

"You did not pay for that yourself," Viktor said in an ominous tone.

"We've come to a different arrangement." She waited until they were in the back of his car to explain. "I promised to put him in contact with my uncle and arrange for some pieces from our curated collection to be sold through this location. It's a win-win. Barsi on Fifth is always looking for ways to expand its visibility."

"What did you say to make him so apologetic after losing a sale that would have paid his lease for months?"

"Oh, you know me and my buses." She tried to sound blasé. "I shamelessly threw you under one. I said you should have explained my connection to the Barsi family and that I'm sure if he'd known we were going to an art museum, he would have steered you toward something with more artistic and conversational value."

His gaze went to the necklace.

"It's made by a local goldsmith. She's still new, but she's managed a very tricky balance—literally. The chain won't slide even though this side of the design has the majority of the stones. I'm quite impressed and will tell every-one what a good eye he has for spotting emerging talent."

"Was it his eye? Or did you educate him on that, too?"

"Are you angry? Viktor, the diamonds aren't *me*. I would have *felt* like a mannequin, with nothing to say except 'Thank you' while people stared at them. I didn't mean to act like a spoiled diva."

"I don't think you're spoiled. Maybe a little," he allowed with a considering tilt of his head. "Who turns up their nose at a small fortune in diamonds? It's some of the most impractical behavior I've witnessed since you climbed into the back of a stranger's car."

"You're laughing at me?" She felt giddily pleased. "I am a snob when it comes to jewelry. You might as well know that up front. But to my mind, this serves the higher purpose of giving me confidence." She traced the edge of the platinum where it had warmed from sitting against her skin.

"You just put two men at the top of their game into their place. How do you need confidence?"

"I mean in my looks and what sort of impression I'll make. Intellectually, I'm fine. I know what I know and I won't let anyone talk me down on that front."

"Who talks down about the way you look? You're beau-tiful."

She shook her head, sorry she'd let her insecurity slip. She had resolved to extend her stay until they knew if she was pregnant, but she hadn't been sure what that meant for them as a couple. There was a lot to unravel there. Thankfully they arrived at their destination, forestalling her having to talk about it.

"I'm not fishing for compliments. Just nervous," she prevaricated.

"You'll be fine." He took her hand. His thumb skated across her opal as he drew her from the car onto the red carpet.

"I don't think you were entirely honest with me," Viktor accused mildly as he drew Rozalia onto the small dance floor a few hours later.

Her step faltered. "When? About what?"

Her shock and indignation were immediate. Predictable, even, making him smile inwardly. He had never met anyone who presented him or herself so candidly.

"You said you don't like attention, but people love talking to you."

"Oh, I can talk about art until people's eyes cross," she dismissed.

Yet, she didn't. Instead, she discovered what interested others and asked about that. She was naturally curious and sought out wallflowers and an elderly woman with a cane who needed help rising and moving closer to inspect the painting. The woman was a patron of the museum, very influential, but that information skimmed past Rozi's radar. She asked about grandchildren and advice on where to buy her mother a gift.

People watched them, which he was used to. His looks and the position he'd held from such a young age had made him a focus for years. His dates usually ate up that attention and ensured he held court the entire night. Other women tended to especially enjoy drawing male attention from all corners, which always niggled, given the betrayal he'd suffered in the past.

With Rozalia at his side, however, he was able to relax. She turned her share of heads, usually with her warm laugh, but didn't seem to notice. She wasn't shy, but quickly gave up the floor to others. It was probably because she came from a big family, but he found it enormously refreshing to be with someone comfortable in who she was without demanding outside validation for it.

It made her remark earlier about not having confidence in her looks all the more puzzling. She might not be the most obviously beautiful woman in the room, but she was definitely the most attractive. He was particularly drawn by his knowledge of how much passionate heat was contained behind her naturally warm smile.

As the craving inside him came more firmly to the fore, he felt as though he might be revealing too much as he held her. His guard was not as firmly in place as he liked, having been disarmed a number of times by her already. He attempted to tamp down on his reaction.

Nevertheless, he couldn't resist trailing his hand to the place where the back of her dress dipped beneath the fall of her hair. He caressed the warm skin he found there, feeling a small quiver go through her as he did.

A growl of approval caught in his throat, nearly released. The golden hoop in her lobe teased him, begging for his head to dip so he could nip lightly at the shell of her exposed ear.

"Viktor, please don't…" She licked her lips and her hand twitched in his.

Had he been squeezing? He shifted his grip, caressing his thumb into her palm to reassure her.

A light flush of pleasure touched her cheeks, enthralling him further.

"I need to know. You said we're dating, but is that merely the impression we're giving? Is tonight just an attempt to change the story in case…?"

In case she was pregnant, she meant.

"Because you said that necklace was a statement," she hurried on. "Which is fine. I realize what you're trying to accomplish publicly, but I need to know what you expect privately."

"That's up to you." He was more than prepared to move back to physical intimacy. Sexual tension continued to simmer closely beneath the surface between them, enticing in the extreme. However, "I'm not taking anything for granted," he assured her.

"Neither am I," she said with a dry chuckle. "That's why I need you to spell it out. Your interest in me has been very transient. I don't want to interpret all these grand gestures of yours as something they're not."

Transient? His interest in her bordered on obsessive.

"Let's continue this conversation in private."

Restless male hunger and some other inscrutable tension lined his expression.

Rozi bit her lip, nervous to be alone with him, but she was feeling too vulnerable to stay here. She'd already been unsure of herself and confused as to where they stood before he'd spent an evening acting like an attentive suitor. His touch just now had brought her insecurity to a head.

She nodded and he drew her back to their table to fetch her purse and say their brief goodbyes. They didn't talk again until they were back at the hotel.

He went directly to the wet bar as they entered their suite, then made a dismissive noise. "I keep forgetting we're not drinking."

"You can drink. It doesn't bother me."

"No, it's just a distraction from a situation I find uncomfortable." He pushed his hands into his pockets and seemed to grapple with his own thoughts and emotions, sounding genuinely remorseful. "I'm not used to being so far in the wrong. I've tried to explain how I've been conditioned to believe everyone has an ulterior motive, but I wish I had handled things better that first night. You have a right to be angry at the things I said. I'm sorry."

"Oh, Viktor. It's not just that," she said on a heavy sigh. "I mean, thank you. I needed to hear that. But I wish I had your skepticism sometimes. I've been stung before, thinking a man was being sincere when he wasn't."

"Who?" he demanded, sounding so affronted she almost thought he was jealous.

"A couple of people I dated." She shrugged it off but stopped short of saying they didn't matter because they did. "I think I've mentioned that Gisella has star power. She doesn't encourage men to slobber all over her, but they do. Some have seen me as a means of getting to her and I only realized that after the fact."

She tried to find an unbothered smile, but felt sick, as if she was peeling back her own skin to reveal how badly she fell short, even though she had worked hard to believe she deserved everything she longed for.

"I try not to be jealous of her," she continued. "But I always have been a little. She was an only child, very well-off, forever wearing designer clothes and getting the latest gadget. The irony is, she would say she's always been jealous of me. Her parents divorced and I told you how she's always felt out of step with the rest of the family. Our mothers are half sisters, but very different. Mine is very supportive and hers is more aloof. I know what I have. I wouldn't give up any of it for her looks and popularity, but I have learned that I'm not the kind of woman men go for."

"These sound like very superficial men you date."

"Some have been, yes. Probably because I'm someone who wants to believe the best in people and wants there to be depth when there is none. But I've learned to be cautious, which is another reason I was still a virgin the other night—and so disappointed afterward."

"Disappointed." He released the word on a breath that seemed to whoosh as though from a body blow.

She swallowed. She wasn't trying to jab at him, just explain.

"Part of me was thinking that at least there was no chance you were actually interested in Gisella, that for once I'd met a man who might actually be interested in *me*."

"That's why you called me a player."

"You behaved like one!" Her fingertips bit into her upper arms as she threw that at him, not sure how he would react.

His cheek ticked. He looked to the bar as though wanting a drink. Made a face.

"It's true that I wasn't thinking ahead to anything more serious than dinner. Certainly not that we'd end up here, contemplating marriage, mere days later."

"I know. And I wasn't anticipating anything this serious, either. But I didn't expect such a big moment for me to be so inconsequential to you."

He closed his eyes in a flinch. When he opened his eyes, his brows came down into a low, thick line, scolding almost. "Surely you've realized by now that the only reason we're in this position is because I was as lost to the experience as you were."

Her heart turned over. She wanted to believe him. Needed to. But, "How could I? I have nothing to compare it to."

"I forgot the condom, Rozalia. I *never* forget." He hooked his hands on his hips. His shaky sigh seemed to rattle his chest, while his expression fought emotion. "But you're right. I should have told you that you were remarkable. You are."

A wave of tingling pleasure suffused her even as mur-

murs of doubt warned her not to get caught up in his be-
lated compliment. These words could be sorcery and the
fancy of her destructively optimistic nature.

"We are remarkable together, Rozi," he stated gravely,
coming toward her to banish every possible qualm with
the magic of his strong hands cradling her face, gentle and
reverential. "If you believe nothing else, believe that I will
never forget that night as long as I live. With or without
anything that has come after, that night will never be inconsequential to *me*. I should have said that then. I should
have…"

His thumbs moved across her cheeks in a troubled caress. He lowered his head to press his mouth to hers, tender and soft. His lips grazed hers in sweeps of remorse
and gratitude and a desire to heal, causing such a sting of
sweetness she flinched.

She was a tactile person, however. A forgiving one. And
someone who felt with her whole body. She stepped into
him on instinct, needing the contact to soothe all the scuffs
and bumps and fears and scorns. He was her only anchor
here in this topsy-turvy world he'd thrown her into, even
though he was also the source of her turmoil. She needed
to hang on to him.

His muscles flexed and he ironed her to his front with
massaging hands, holding her close as they both shuddered
under a rush of emotion. His hands moved in a twitchy
soothe as he rubbed her back.

Their chaste kiss tremored toward passion.

He started to lift his head and she dove her fingers into
his hair, urging him to stay close enough to continue their
kiss. She was the one who let it slide into something more
erotic by tilting her head to deepen the fit, parting her lips
farther, inviting him to ravage.

He started to, the hunger in him a flash fire that wanted to consume her.

With a sudden, jagged noise, he lifted his head, nostrils flaring as he sucked in a harsh breath.

"Be sure," he commanded in a gruff tone. "You kiss me like that and I'll lose my head again." He made it sound like such a dire threat even as he tucked her hair behind her ear in a simple, unexpected caress that left her quivering.

She wasn't sure of anything, but she wanted to be sure of him. Of this—that she had an effect on him that equaled the one he had on her.

If that much was true, she hoped it meant she could affect him in other ways. Ways that would lead him to expose his heart to her. She hoped, desperately, deliriously hoped, that this was the foundation of her future with this man.

And if she didn't have one, at least she would have this. A memory.

She tested his warning by tightening her arms around his neck and rising onto her toes. Then she pressed her mouth to the one that occupied so many of her erotic dreams and felt him stiffen slightly.

He set light hands behind her waist but let her continue to play. Allowed her to flagrantly indulge herself— to run her hands into his hair and kiss the corners of his mouth and slide her tongue along the smooth fullness of his bottom lip. She caught that sinful piece of him between her teeth as though it was exotic fruit and lightly pulled, forcing the sexiest noise she'd ever heard to emit from his throat.

He was hard, she discovered, as she leaned her weight into him. It made her want to laugh with the heady power she had over him. She skimmed her nibbling mouth across the hardness of his jaw into the flesh in his throat, fingers digging at his collar to expose more of him to her busy mouth.

With another primal noise, he sent the world tilting off its axis as he scooped her into the cradle of his arms against his chest. "You sound sure."

She threw back her head in surrender as he carried her to the bedroom.

CHAPTER EIGHT

HE TOOK HER to his room and stood her beside his bed.

"Do we use one of these this time?" he asked, taking a box from the night table.

"The hotels in America keep Bibles in that drawer."

"There are times, Rozalia, when I am capable of optimism. I put them there earlier." He peeled off his tuxedo jacket.

She could feel her lips quivering with humor, but also nerves. Anticipation and excitement, but shards of uncertainty. He was still so much more experienced than she was. So broad and strong, shoulders flexing as he twisted out of his shirt to reveal his chest. Intimidating.

Yet so gorgeously built of smooth contours and a light texture of hair, two dark nipples standing tight with excitement. Her hand went out to touch before she realized what she was doing. Crisp hair turned to damp satin beneath her fingertips as she traced the line down the center of his chest to the stacked muscles in his abdomen.

"I wish I was a sculptor," she murmured.

"This is better," he said, catching her hand and drawing it to his mouth. "I want to touch you, too. Feel every inch. Taste and savor."

He bit erotically against the heel of her palm, making clear to her that this was the reason she was so unnerved right now. Her reaction to him was a deep, dark river of feelings that were still new, yet so strong she couldn't control them. Her trembles increased and her eyes dampened with longing—from one teasing, innocuous bite and the graze of his lips against the unsteady pulse in her wrist.

He wasn't shaking like this, weak in the knees and growing overwhelmed. Was he?

She splayed her hand on his ribs, seeking to ground herself, but he took it as a signal of some kind and tangled his hand in her hair, dragging her close to claim her mouth with nearly bruising hunger.

Thick, potent craving swirled through her, so heavy and hot she could hardly bear the rush of it in her veins. The sensual need that gathered between her thighs was so acute she groaned in agony.

He tore his mouth off hers and dropped his head against her shoulder, wide shoulders lifting in heaving pants as he held her in the tense cage of his arms.

"I didn't mean to hurt you," he said in a gritty voice. "I'm trying to take this slow."

With a type of wonder, she drifted her fingertips across his muscled chest and shoulders, discovering smooth, intriguing dips and lovely sensitive spots that made him flex in reaction.

"It hurts when you stop," she whispered.

"Don't tell me that," he groaned, turning his head to bury his mouth against her neck. He dragged hot, wet kisses along her nape, shooting pleasurable tingles through her whole body that detonated in the tips of her breasts.

She bit her lip as she whimpered in helplessness. But there was no stopping now. She dipped her chin to find his mouth with her own and they held that fused kiss as they both fumbled at the fastening of her gown.

She didn't let his adeptness impact her, too grateful

for the loosening of the silk, the coolness of the air as the fabric fell away.

He lifted his head to peruse her while she stood before him in a strapless bra and panties, heels and the amethyst necklace.

Feminine power rose within her as his gaze fixated, yet shifted over her, as though determined to memorize every shadowed curve and rosy swell of her form. She lifted her hands to remove the clips from her hair, taking her time sliding the clips free and letting them fall with a faint thud against the puddled dress. Then she finger-combed her hair, enjoying the way he watched, mesmerized.

In another brazen move, she released her bra and let it fall away, breathing with deep relief at being freed from the restraint.

His hands came up to replace the cups of white lace, both soothing and inciting as he warmed and lifted, plumping and skimming his thumbs across the turgid tips.

She held very still, gripped by the need for his touch, but the sensation was so intense, she locked her hands around his wrists and made a tortured noise.

"Too much?" he asked through gritted teeth, lifting his gaze so she could read the wildness in his eyes. The animal he was barely containing. "Or not enough?" He trailed one hand down to slide unerringly beneath the front of her underpants.

Wordless sounds came out of her as his fingertips sawed and parted, seeking the point that sent stars shooting behind her eyelids before she'd even realized she had closed her eyes. He dipped lower, laying claim with a tender penetration that she clung to in a clench of joyous welcome.

His mouth covered hers, stealing what breath she had as he continued caressing, tripping her into a sudden, electric orgasm that took them both by surprise at its swift ferocity. She cried out and clung to him, so overcome her knees gave out.

He embraced her tenderly as he nibbled at her ear and spoke soothing words against her cheek and neck. "You are determined to drive me out of my mind, aren't you?"

"Me?" Did he realize how thoroughly he had just undone her?

"I want you so badly, I'm coming out of my skin and I haven't come *near* everything I want to do to you."

"I don't know if I can take more than that," she said even as wantonness husked her voice.

"We'll find out, won't we?" His grin was feral and full of wicked intention as he skimmed his hand down to drop her panties off her hips and nudged her backward toward the edge of the mattress. "Lie down." He tracked his gaze over her, tightening wires of anticipation in her.

"Wait." Holding his gaze, she worked to open his belt and fly, watching a snarl of intense arousal harden his expression.

She looked down as she hitched his pants off his hips, baring the jut of his arousal. Her hands were drawn to touch this part of him as much as the rest. His shape was utterly fascinating, the responsiveness of him an aphrodisiac. Her tongue moistened in her mouth as she explored him with a light touch, inner muscles clenching afresh with need.

With a helpless look up at him, she could only plead, "Viktor."

"You're not aroused enough. I might hurt you."

She choked on a laugh and showed him how her hand shook. "I'm dying."

Growling a noise that sounded like an animal in pain, he kicked out of his clothes and sat on the edge of the bed.

"Come here, then." He reached for a condom and applied it, then drew her to stand on her knees straddling his thighs.

He teased her, locking an arm around her waist so her breasts pouted invitingly at his mouth. He sucked one and the other, going back and forth while his free hand caressed the back of her thigh and her cheeks and toyed where she wept with need for him.

She wriggled with deepening urgency and scraped her fingers through the gloss of his hair and across his shoulders.

"Viktor!" she commanded—begged, catching handfuls of his hair to tip back his head, growing rough with her rising anxiety. She was feverish, totally governed by the need that gripped her. The primitive huntress that lurked inside her edged past rational thought and civilized behavior to call to her mate. *"I need you."*

His pupils dilated and he bared his teeth in what might have been a triumphant grin if his jaw wasn't pulsing with the tension of slipping restraint.

"Now you understand," he said grittily.

For a few taut seconds, they teetered on the atavistic line between human and animal. His hands shifted heavily to her hips. She slid her own between them, guiding the crest of him to her entrance as she lowered herself.

There was no pain, only the sensual breach of him filling her as she settled into his lap, inner thighs burning at the stretch, the rest of her arching in sensual luxury. His hands skimmed over her and they kissed long and deep.

She took up a smooth, controlled rhythm, one that made their hearts seem to beat in unison. It was sweaty and glorious and earthy and all consuming. She couldn't have held back if she wanted to. They were too intimately positioned, eye to eye, mouth to mouth, a light friction between their chests, hands free to roam and grasp and steal intimate caresses.

Rather than let her grow frantic as her pitch of arousal neared breaking point, he set firm hands on her hips.

"Not yet," he whispered, nipping at her chin, then sucking hard enough on her neck to sting. The tip of his tongue circled to soothe, driving her crazy. "Feel."

She wanted to cry, but she slowed to savor each dazzling retreat and return. It was such an exhilarating but profound state, she opened her eyes to tell him, but didn't have to say a word. She read the same glaze of abandonment to passion in his eyes. Could hear his control hanging by a thread in the way his breath caught and his tense hand pressed into her tailbone.

She was stunned to realize she was giving him the same experience. They undulated in this state of bliss together, each brought here by the other. Soul mates.

The quivering shock waves of climax gathered with a final, irresistible twist, releasing in a flourish of pleasurable contractions that turned her vision to white light and filled her ears with the rush of the sea.

She would have mourned her loss of control if she hadn't felt his arms tighten around her, drawing her deep onto him as he pulsed heat within her. His ragged sounds of anguished joy came to her from a distance as the storm of convulsive ecstasy held them in its grip.

Gradually his most intense shudders abated to light aftershocks, allowing Viktor's consciousness to absorb that he was still holding Rozi in his lap. He caressed her back as his chest shook and he tried to calm his breathing. The pillow of her breast didn't mute the unsteady pound of her heartbeat. He could feel it rocking her while fine shivers continued to chase over her.

He had thought their first experience extraordinary, but this had superseded it by miles. No other woman had ever undermined his control and transported him this way. She was the most potent drug imaginable and his rational mind sounded a full-scale alarm of potential self-destruction if he continued to indulge himself with her.

Then her fingertips moved in a light caress in the hollow at the base of his skull and he let his eyes drift shut. He sank back into the soporific high she provided, twisting so he had her beneath him on the mattress.

They kissed lazily until he had to withdraw.

"Don't move. I'll be right back." He disposed of the condom in the bathroom and returned to find she'd shifted onto her side and drawn a pillow under her head.

She was a creamy nude bathed in apricot light, exquisite and heavy-lidded with satiation. But the way she sought his gaze with her own made his heart lurch. That shadow of yearning in her eyes told him she was looking for a reassurance beyond the physical. An emotional connection.

That did alarm him. Even without his brother's betrayal, he'd never been one for deep relationships. He simply wasn't built that way.

He settled facing her, letting his hand roam the curve of her hip as he kissed the point of her shoulder. She sighed and her hand draped against his neck, easing the tension rooting inside him. They fit together like two pieces of a puzzle and kissed purely for the enjoyment of it.

He couldn't give this up. Wouldn't.

But he couldn't give her what she wanted, either.

It was a contradiction he didn't know how to resolve.

"Gisella is asking me why you're sending Kaine money." Gisella was asking her a lot of things that Rozi didn't know how to answer. She had put her off by saying they were traveling to see Viktor's aunt Bella, which was true, but she would have to confess all to her soon.

She didn't know where to start, though. Admitting she had slept with Viktor was a big enough deal but telling her cousin she had risked pregnancy would push Gisella into full-protection mode. She might get on a plane, or worse, tell one of their mothers.

"You said you didn't want her indebted to Kaine Michaels for covering your legal bills," Viktor replied. "I'm the one responsible regardless."

"But I'm worried about her. She seems to be spending a lot of time with him. She was so furious when he got the earring at that auction and he hasn't even shown it to her. I'm mad at myself now that I didn't ask you if I could send her a photo of the one you have."

"You can spend more time studying it when we return to Budapest. Take all the photos you like."

"You don't mind? I'd love that. Thank you."

He was such a confounding man. The minute she began to think he was growing disinterested, he would do something to flip her view of him. They had just spent two days at his flat in Vienna. He'd worked long hours at his office during the day, leaving her with a credit card and a command to buy outfits for a list of appearances over the next two weeks. She had poked around various shops, enjoying the history of the city but growing homesick and lonely being on her own.

Then he'd surprised her with a privately chartered river cruise to Visegrád, where his aunt lived. He continued working off his laptop, disappearing to take conference calls a few times a day, but he spent a lot of time with her, too. They went ashore to visit sites the moment she expressed an interest, dined by candlelight while the sky streaked with pink and mauve and talked idly as they watched the scenic shoreline of the Danube drift past.

It was like a honeymoon, she kept thinking, except there'd been no ring and no declaration of love.

What were his feelings? she wondered. Was he falling the way she was? Part of her worried her feelings were simply the excitement of being with such a gorgeous specimen of a man. Who wouldn't tumble headlong for someone who looked that good? One who paid for a private cruise on short notice and made her feel sensual and sexual and special?

She had no such appeal to offer. She was ordinary and, at best, could make him a ring that matched his inscrutable personality.

After five days, the castle on the hill above Visegrád came into view. She was instantly charmed and insisted Viktor come out of their stateroom to stand at the rail and see it with her.

"Are you purposely making me feel as though I live in a fairy tale?" she asked.

"I'm always amused when I visit America and they proudly show off a historic building that is 'over a hundred years old.' Call me when you get to a thousand," he dismissed with his dry sense of humor.

"I'm excited to meet your aunt, but I'm sorry to leave this. It's been lovely. Thank you." She slid her arms around his waist, comfortable taking such liberties with him after a week of constant lovemaking.

"It's been my pleasure," he assured her, mouth twitching with memory of what they'd been doing only a short hour ago. Her own mouth had been learning new things that had wrung groans of ecstasy from him.

She blushed recalling it but shivered with delight as he skimmed her hair back from her neck and kissed the skin he exposed. Then she rested her head on his shoulder as the boat landing drew closer.

It shouldn't have felt so ominous, but she found herself tightening her hold on him. What if he was right about her grandmother stealing the earrings? She still didn't believe it, but worried that whatever she learned would impact what she'd managed to build with him. They were so fragile and new. She didn't know how much weather they could take without being torn apart.

Viktor's mother had been scheduled to go back to Budapest, but once she had heard he wanted to bring Rozi to see Aunt Bella, she had opted to stay and meet her, as well. Viktor couldn't fault Mara Rohan for wanting to meet Rozalia, especially given the Trudi debacle, but he would rather she kept her nose out. Things were falling into place and he felt inordinately protective of what they had. His mother could be hard to take and he didn't want Rozi's tender feelings impacted.

"You don't like it?" Rozi asked as she appeared in a sundress with a floral print. It wasn't tailored, but it was tasteful and fit her beautifully. Even so, his mother would likely call it *bohemian*. Rozi's loose hair and sun-kissed innocence were the complete opposite of the overgroomed sophisticates his mother always tried to steer him toward.

His mother was an unapologetic elitist. She never missed an opportunity to point out that she had married a count and, if things were different, would be eligible for the title of countess.

"You look lovely," he assured Rozi, clearing his thoughts from his expression.

"Oh, this is charming," she said a short while later as they approached the villa through his aunt's small vineyard.

The grounds were well kept, the house modernized by

his aunt over the years into a welcoming manor from the tomb-like ancestral seat he recalled from his visits as a child.

They were shown into the garden where his mother and aunt were situated on outdoor sofas, bright silk cushions tucked around them and a gazebo providing them shade. A fountain trickled nearby.

His aunt was quiet-natured and reclusive, but still quite elegant, always wearing a skirt and keeping her white hair in a tidy bun. His mother wore one of her couture skirt-and-jacket sets, her yellow collar popped so the points emphasized the strength in her jaw and the sharpness of her blue-green eyes.

"I didn't think I could be more enchanted by the land of my roots, but I find myself in awe once again," Rozi said to his aunt as he made the introductions. "Your garden is truly magical. A perfect place to relax and recuperate. I hope your ankle is improving?"

"It is. Thank you," Aunt Bella said, visibly warming to Rozi.

Viktor caught his mother's raised brow as she silently questioned his sharing family details with a stranger.

Niceties passed as Rozi asked after this or that flower and accepted a glass of lemonade. His mother waited until they were seated at the table for a meal overlooking the koi pond to take control of the conversation.

"I was quite surprised to learn there was anyone in America claiming to be related. All these years and never an inquiry."

"You're family from America?" Aunt Bella's gaze sharpened on Rozi. Clearly his mother hadn't warned her.

"We're still trying to establish that," his mother said with a flat, frosted smile.

"*I'm* not family," Rozi said, touching her chest. "My

cousin Gisella was supposed to come. She asked her mother, Alisz, if she wanted to accompany her. Alisz would be your niece," she said to Bella. "And your cousin," she said with a nod to Mara. "But her summer lecture schedule was already in place. She's very well respected in academic circles in America. We have always assumed that was Istvan's genes. The rest of us are more artsy, not nearly the intellectual that she is."

"Istvan was terribly smart," Bella agreed distantly, brows pulled into a frown of old grief and fresh consternation.

"We would need a blood test to determine whether this aunt of yours is *actually* Istvan's daughter," Mara reminded stiffly. "You would think she would have come forward before now if she is."

"My grandfather, Benedek, always treated her very much as though she was his own. He was the only father she knew and she thought it would be disrespectful to him to search out blood ties with her biological father's family while he was alive. After he passed, she was beyond having any curiosity about it. You probably wouldn't have heard from any of us if her daughter, Gisella, and I weren't obsessed with the earrings."

"The ones that were stolen," Mara said pointedly. "Am I to understand your cousin is in San Francisco right now, attempting to acquire what rightfully belongs to us?"

"Kaine Michaels bought it fair and square," Viktor pointed out. Although, the man's method had been a sledgehammer to a thumb tack, buying the whole damned estate in one fell swoop, locking Viktor's representative out of the opportunity to bid at all.

Viktor had since had a message from Michaels that his fight wasn't with him, but the missed chance was still annoying as hell.

"I don't believe my grandmother did steal them," Rozi said. "She's simply not like that. I don't know how the story got so turned around."

"The story came straight from my mother," Mara said, chilly and pointed. "She had it directly from her own mother. The earrings were stolen by a young woman who claimed to have a relationship with Istvan. She sold one in Budapest to pay for passage to America with her husband. That one made its way to my late mother-in-law. She gave it to me as a wedding gift. The other was sold in America and sat in a private collection for years until it surfaced a few months ago, when I asked Viktor to purchase it for me."

"Oh, gosh, that's not correct at all! Grandmamma wasn't married when she went to America. She didn't marry my grandfather until after my aunt Alisz was born. Istvan gave her the earrings and she sold one to pay for her passage. When she ran out of money in America, she sold the second one to my grandfather. She was alone with a new baby and he was opening his shop. They decided to marry and open the shop together. But she didn't steal the earrings. Istvan gave them to her as an engagement promise. He was going to meet her in America and marry her there."

"You're *wrong*," his mother began.

"Your grandmother is Eszti!" Bella said in a tone of shocked discovery.

Viktor wished he'd been watching his aunt, rather than closely monitoring whether his mother was upsetting Rozi. Aunt Bella was quite pale now, having taken in the nature of the controversy.

"Yes!" Rozi said with her brightest smile. "Grandmamma was Eszti Miska before she married Benedek Barsi. Do you remember her?"

"Oh, I see so much of her in you now. Oh, goodness."

Aunt Bella smiled mistily, fingers going to her throat. "Oh, yes, of course! She was such a lovely, warm, charming young woman. It was never any wonder to me why Istvan fell so hard for her. How is she?"

"Excellent. She was ill this winter but she's recovering well. That's why Gisella and I have been anxious to find the earrings and buy them back for her. She genuinely loved your brother. I know she'll be so happy if she can at least hold the gift he gave her."

"But he didn't give them to her," Mara insisted sharply.

"No," Bella agreed. Her expression fell into anguished lines. "I did."

CHAPTER NINE

"I DON'T UNDERSTAND." Viktor's mother's eyes narrowed while Bella's welled.

"I promised Viktor I wouldn't upset you." Rozi reached out to cover the older woman's hand, feeling awful for distressing her. She seemed so nice and welcoming. "I'm so sorry. It must be a painful time to remember."

"Very," Bella agreed, squeezing back weakly. "And the lie was necessary at the time, but the truth would serve better today. Your mother only knew what our mother told our father," Bella said to Mara. "Irenke was staying with friends that weekend."

Irenke was Mara's mother and the sister Bella shared with Istvan.

"She was called home when it was confirmed that Istvan had been killed in one of the demonstrations."

Rozi set her other hand over their joined ones, bracing the older woman for the return of what she could see were agonizing memories.

"I longed to tell Irenke what had really happened, but she was always very outspoken. I was afraid she would confront our father and he might very well have killed her himself if she went against him. He was a hard man. Heartless, at times. He and Istvan had terrible arguments. I've never been sure if Istvan joined the demonstrations out of genuine principle or simply to flout our father."

She reached for her lemonade. Her hand shook as she sipped and swallowed.

"Our parents had been out for the evening. They had just arrived home when Eszti arrived. I went to the top of the stairs because I heard the shouting. Mother was crying. Father must have slapped Eszti. She was crying and holding her cheek." Bella set her hand against her own cheek. "He called her a liar. Other terrible things. He threw her out. Then he told Mother to stop crying. He said, 'He's not dead. He can't be.'" Bella moved her hand to her heart.

Rozi was totally focused on the older woman, unable to tear her eyes off her to see how Mara and Viktor were reacting.

"Mother came up the stairs and the look in her eyes... I knew Istvan was gone. I thought I would die myself. She said, *That girl said she's carrying his baby.* Mother took off her earrings and put them in my hand." Bella showed her empty palm. "She told me to go after her. To tell her to take Istvan's baby somewhere safe. I caught Eszti at the gate. It was raining. We were both crying. She loved him so much. We hugged, but I had to get back before my father noticed I was outside. I never saw her again."

She took another sip of lemonade, gaze slowly coming back from the past to rest on Rozi.

"The next time Mother was meant to wear the earrings was after the funeral. She told my father she had taken off her earrings when they entered the house, that she had left them on the table and Eszti must have taken them. It wasn't until Dorika paid a visit to our parents to arrange your marriage that I learned Eszti had sold one for passage to America." Bella spoke to Mara. "I've always wondered if there really was a baby."

"Let me show you some photos of Aunt Alisz and Gisella." Rozi quickly flicked through her phone and handed it to Bella.

"Oh, Mara, look. Tell me those aren't your eyes." She handed the phone to Mara.

The thick tension began to ease, but Rozi was left in a small cloud of melancholy. They talked a little more over their perfectly civil lunch. Bella was curious about the shop and Rozi made a point of showing off her ring. "Gisella made it. She's extremely talented."

Mara was less enthused, making a noncommittal noise that was so like one of Aunt Alisz's lukewarm reactions, Rozi bit back a laugh.

"Show her the one you made for Gisella," Viktor prompted, something in his tone telling her he knew his mother would prefer it.

"You made that?" Mara asked as she looked down her nose at the screen. "It's eye-catching."

Faint praise, but Rozi was pleased to earn it.

As they lingered over their coffee, Bella said she wanted to rest.

"Viktor will help you," Mara said in a blatantly undis-guised attempt to have some time alone with Rozi.

Viktor shot her a look as he rose to help his aunt.

Rozi smiled, not intimidated in the least.

"Do stay the night," Bella urged Rozi. "I'd like to hear more about your aunt and cousin."

"If Viktor can spare the time, of course."

Mara narrowed her eyes as the two disappeared into the house. "Exactly what are you hoping to accomplish?" she asked bluntly.

"My goal was to buy the earring for my grandmother.

I realize now that would cause her more pain than she already carries. That's not your concern, though. Is it? You want to know if I have designs on Viktor."

"I'm quite sure you do."

Honestly, she was so much like Aunt Alisz, Rozi was struck with an urge to laugh with familiarity and cry with homesickness at the same time.

"We have a running joke in our family that Aunt Alisz is the one you go to for the advice you don't want to hear. She's very dispassionate in her delivery, but always has our family's best interests at heart."

"Bella is the one with the interest in your aunt and cousin," Mara reminded with a cool smile.

"That was my attempt to varnish my reply," Rozi clarified, tone as gentle as she could make it. "My intention is to let Viktor make up his own mind about me. I think it would be best for your relationship with him if you did the same."

A handful of subtle emotions flickered across Mara's expression. Affront, a shadow of guilt and pain. Sadness, and a sharper suspicion.

"We're talking about the incident with Trudi? I will take some responsibility for her making certain assumptions about Viktor's intentions. I had no idea she was capable of taking such a juvenile action. That's extremely unfortunate and I regret how you were treated."

"She owes me an apology. You don't," Rozi said, deliberately magnanimous. "And I can appreciate that having lost one son, you're committed to securing Viktor's future. That, like any mother, you want to see him settled and producing grandchildren. And perhaps you feel you owe some extra care and attention to helping him find a suitable partner, given how things turned out in the past."

Mara looked to the side, profile stiff. "Well, he has been confiding, hasn't he?"

"The other thing we say about Aunt Alisz is that she wears her heart *up* her sleeve, not on it, but it doesn't mean she doesn't have one."

"Yes, well, I'm sure Viktor would not say the same about me." She took a sip of her lemonade and there was only the tiniest shift in the ice cubes. She set down the glass. "It was a difficult time after his father died. His brother was having trouble taking on such a level of responsibility. I thought a supportive wife would help. Hindsight is twenty-twenty, but at the time I believed she and Kristof were the better match. Had I realized Viktor would never forgive me, I would have acted differently."

Rozi didn't bother stating that *this* was Mara's opportunity to act differently. She seemed like an intelligent woman.

Besides, Viktor emerged from the house and rejoined them. The conversation turned to other things.

Viktor caught his mother alone before dinner. He poured her wine and handed it to her, then waited for the inevitable barrage of disapproval.

"You're not joining me?" she asked.

"I'll wait for Rozi." She'd gone up to change for dinner but seemed to be taking a long time.

"She said she would put me in touch with a watchmaker who could fix your grandmother's watch so I could wear it again."

"She's quite passionate about vintage jewelry."

"She's different from your usual type."

"If we're comparing her to Trudi, or any of the other women you've earmarked for me, yes. Very." She wasn't even much like the young woman he'd once been so infatuated with. That girl had been from the right family with the smooth, aloof charm provided by a Swiss education. He couldn't honestly remember what had attracted him so inexorably, only how crushed he had been that his brother had betrayed him and that his mother had been instrumental in turning her against him.

Which made sharp talons of protectiveness rise under his skin as he regarded his mother, awaiting her judgment on Rozi. If she had any thoughts of driving a wedge between them…

She caught his hard stare and lifted a negligent brow.

"I wouldn't call it the most advantageous connection. Nor would it be the least. I wouldn't be *un*happy if you decided you were serious about her."

"Try not to gush, Mother. You're embarrassing both of us," he drawled. At least she'd taken him at his word to remove herself from matchmaking.

His aunt arrived and he poured for her, then decided to go in search of Rozi. He found her dressed, but sitting on the edge of the bed, pale and shocked.

"What's wrong?" He looked to the phone on the night table. "Bad news?"

"I threw up," she said, sounding dazed. "I felt fine one minute, then it hit me like a train."

"Food poisoning? You ate what I ate." He touched her forehead and cheeks. Her skin was cool and damp, her hair was wet around her hairline, her makeup scrubbed clean. But she didn't feel feverish. She smelled of toothpaste and her color was coming back.

"I don't know." Her fretful gaze met his.

"Morning sickness?" He sat down beside her, head swimming as possibility became probability. "It's evening." He found himself trying to manage his expectations, so he wouldn't be let down. "You haven't even taken a test. When do symptoms usually start?"

"I don't know." Her expression was bewildered. "I know it's usually worse in the first trimester. I'll look it up later. It's probably something else."

He took her hand, finding her palm clammy. "Do you want to stay here and rest?"

"I feel fine now." She sounded exasperated. "But what if it's a virus? I don't want to get your aunt sick."

"I think we both know it's not a virus. *I'm* not sick." They spent a lot of time with their lips locked, breathing each other's panted breaths.

"No," she agreed faintly.

"You should eat something. If you can." The shields of protectiveness that had been pushing out of him and forming around her over the last week developed a second, softer layer. He wanted to full-on coddle her.

She nodded and came downstairs with him.

The evening passed pleasantly with Rozi relaxing as the sickness seemed to have abated. She filled his aunt's ears with stories about her aunt's and cousin's accomplishments. Even his mother seemed interested as Rozi described the work they did at the shop.

Viktor listened with half an ear, reconfiguring things in his mind as he began accepting the reality of a wife and child.

"Were we keeping you from work?" Rozi asked when they retired to their room for the night. "You seemed distracted."

"I was thinking about your work, actually. Do you intend to keep it up if you're pregnant?"

"What?" The tension around her eyes returned. "I haven't thought about that at all."

"*Can* you work pregnant? Are there chemicals or other dangers?"

Her eyes grew bright with concern.

"I wear masks, mostly for dust, but a special one for fumes if I'm soldering. The workshop has to be properly ventilated, too. That's the, um, tricky part, I suppose." She swiped the back of her wrist across her eyebrow. "I would have to check out the different shops in Budapest, see if anyone is looking for a goldsmith. But I'm not ready to think about that, Viktor. We don't *know*."

"But we *should* think about it. I can help you set up a shop at home or somewhere in the city. Could the conservatory be converted, do you think? Either way, you have lots of choices."

"No, I don't! That's why I'm panicking!"

It struck him that she really hadn't expected to be pregnant.

He bit back a chuckle, not sure where the urge to laugh came from. It was definitely a bad idea to imply that her distress amused him. It didn't, but there was a swell inside him somewhere between pride and exaltation. He had to temper an urge to pick her up and spin her around.

He settled for cupping her face in his hands and pressing his mouth over her trembling lips in a warm, lingering kiss, trying to convey that she was safe. He would look after her.

She reacted the way she always did, as though she couldn't get enough of him. She released an indulgent moan into his mouth. The sound echoed in his ears, causing his own response to double down. He took control, shifted his hands to cradle the back of her head as he ravaged her mouth, bordering on rough, but she gave back the same insatiable, mind-blowing passion.

With another whimper of frantic hunger, she slid her hands up his chest and around his neck, pulling him down into the kiss as she threw herself against him.

Just as quickly, she cried out in pain and jerked back, startling him into dropping his hands onto her hips, steadying both of them. Her eyes had welled.

"*Drágám*, what—?" He had never used the endearment in his life, but he was struck with bewilderment that he had caused her pain. He needed her to know it wasn't intentional.

"That hurt. A *lot*." She splayed her hands protectively over the swells of her breasts. "I noticed they were getting tender and thought it was PMS." The corners of her mouth trembled and dipped. "But they've never hurt this bad and—" She covered her face. "Oh, Viktor. It's another symptom."

"Rozi." He drew her in for a gentle embrace, taking care to let her keep her arms between them so she could protect her chest from another painful squashing. He rubbed her back, but she remained tense. He finally stroked her hair and kissed her temple.

"We don't have to make love if you don't want to."

"But I *want* to make love. I just don't want my chest to hurt. It's frustrating."

He was back to smiling and burying it in her hair so she wouldn't think he was laughing at her when he was simply delighted by her. He drew her into his lap as he sat on the edge of the bed and held her as though she was made of spun glass, inhaling the scent in her hair.

"If you want to make love, I will always find a way," he promised her, nuzzling her ear and working his way toward the mouth that he was hungry to plunder again. "You know how I adore your breasts. I'll miss sucking your nipples. You seem to like that as much as I do. But there are other places I like to put my mouth."

She made a restive noise and shifted on his thighs, responding to his suggestive talk. He let his fingers trail over her knee and drew teasing circles on the sensitive skin of her inner thigh.

"Places that drive you wild."

Her breathing was changing and she was trying to catch at his mouth with her own.

"Tell me what you want," he commanded, rubbing his lips into her throat. He trailed kisses down to her breast-bone and lightly nudged her knees farther apart, so he could stretch long fingers up to the hot silk between.

"You know," she said, arms around his neck, teeth sharp on his earlobe before she soothed the pain by sucking, making his scalp tingle.

He did let her see his savage smile then, lifting his head to watch her as he traced his finger against silk that was growing damp. "Tell me you want my mouth *here*." She was trembling, lips parted and eyelashes fluttering as her focus tried to balance between his distracting touch and his commanding voice. "You know I do."

"Say it." He was going out of his mind with this little game, as aroused by the tease as she was. "I don't want to hurt you. You have to tell me everything you want me to do to you."

She shifted, arched, tried to open her legs and invite an increase in pressure. "Please, Viktor." She ran her tongue around his ear, nearly sending his eyes into the back of his head. "Make love to me with your mouth and your hands and *this*."

Her hand went down his abdomen, finding his shape behind his fly and squeezing. He was so hard and ready, he nearly exploded.

He shifted her onto her back on the mattress and flipped her skirt up to her stomach. Then he snapped her under-pants at the hip with a wrench of his wrist, leaving the torn scrap on the floor as he sank to his knees. One long wet lick up the inside of one thigh, then the other, had her quivering in readiness. Her scent intoxicated him, driving him to the edge of his control.

But as much as he wanted to throw himself on top of her and drive them both off the edge into ecstasy, he wanted *this*. Her utter surrender to his care of her. He wanted her to know she was safe in her vulnerability to him. That he would look after her in every possible way.

Stretching his hand across her abdomen, he held her flat when she writhed under his pleasuring, urging her to endure it. He reveled in the way she muffled her cries of joy with her wrist. Then he did it again. And caressed her until the sharp pinnacle of climax stole her control a third time.

He hesitated briefly then, before he put on a condom. He was convinced they didn't need the protection. She was his now. He *knew* it and wanted *her* to know it.

He used one, though, then moved onto the bed, staying on his knees between hers as he thrust into her, holding himself above her so he wouldn't hurt her tender, beautiful breasts.

She was on her back below him, all glazed eyes and hair clinging to her damp temples. She licked her swollen lips so they were shiny and inviting. She arched her neck in luxuriant joy. "Never stop," she breathed, and locked her heels into his buttocks, urging him to drive deep and stay there.

He bared his teeth, turned on beyond bearing when she fought his withdrawal with her feminine strength, inner muscles clinging to keep him from retreating.

He set his fists into the mattress beside her rib cage and let his hips meet hers heavily, watching to ensure she was with him.

"You're mine," he told her, hearing himself at a distance

and wondering where this barbarian had come from. Still, he insisted she confirm it. "Say it."

She moved her arms across the covers as though making angels and bit her lip.

He slowed his strokes and used his thumb to caress where they were joined, teasing her, circling the knot of nerves that made her thighs tense and her breath catch.

"Say it."

"I am," she groaned in capitulation. "I'm yours. All yours."

Words were impossible after that. It was all he could do to keep from becoming a true savage. He ensured he didn't hurt her, but a primal need to imprint himself on her overtook him and she came with him. She used the leverage of her feet in his ass to meet his thrusts and twisted in erotic agony right before his vision went red and his heart exploded. For long seconds, he felt nothing but wave after wave of ecstasy.

Slowly he let himself wilt next to her, breathing ragged, eyes too heavy to open.

Rozi had been sure…quite, quite sure…that she wouldn't be pregnant. This sojourn with Viktor was just a poignantly sweet side trip she would carry into old age as a youthful memory. His talk of her marrying him and setting up her own shop in the conservatory and raising her child in a foreign land away from her family was talk, that's all.

For all her romantic notions, she was a very ordinary person. Big things didn't happen to her. She *preferred* vanilla ice cream and blue jeans and even preferred to listen to middle-of-the-road music like adult contemporary or country pop.

So even though she bolted out of Viktor's arms first

thing in the morning and threw up violently enough to alarm him, she refused to believe she was pregnant.

He insisted on taking her to the doctor in Visegrád that morning, though, while she insisted on looking up exotic diseases that might cause abnormal breast tenderness and nausea without a fever.

"A negative could be a false negative," the doctor warned when he realized she hadn't even missed her cycle yet. "But a positive is almost certainly a positive."

Even now, armed with that warning, as the doctor sat across from her wearing his white coat and a pleasant yet very much *not* joking look on his face, and said the words, "You're pregnant," she was still thinking, *But it could be norovirus.*

The doctor prescribed prenatal vitamins. Viktor promised to find her a family doctor in Budapest for routine screenings and ongoing pregnancy care. Rozi tried to think of any other time they had forgotten contraception beyond that very first time and bit her tongue against asking if it was *really* possible that it only took the once?

They left his aunt's home as soon as they could without arousing suspicions. His mother was staying with his aunt until her ankle improved so it was only the two of them in the back of Viktor's chauffeured car as they continued on their journey.

She didn't realize she was working her ring against her knuckle until Viktor's hand covered hers. He wove his fingers through hers and said, "You're going to bruise yourself."

She flexed her hand in his. "I honestly didn't think it would happen."

"And you're unhappy?"

"No! I'm worried…" She made herself look at him. She'd been avoiding that, too afraid to see suspicions had returned or some other accusatory emotion.

He wore a look she could hardly describe. His features were sharp with alert tension, but the kind that came from anticipation. Like a racehorse ready to bolt out of its gate. Dynamic excitement came off him in such radiant waves, she was fairly blinded by the glow.

"You're happy," she said in stunned comprehension.

"I am."

"But now you have to marry me."

"Yes." His hooded eyes watched her. "And you have to marry me."

A giddy coil sprang in her with a jolt of excitement. "You want that?"

"I do."

Now she was going to fall apart again, chin crinkling and mouth unsteady as her emotions wobbled.

"When?"

He brushed the back of his knuckle under her eye where a single tear had blinked onto her cheekbone.

"I looked up a few things myself, you know," he teased lightly. "I'm to expect mood swings. And a woman who is rightly overwhelmed by the changes going on inside and around her."

"Everything is changing."

"True. So you tell me. A big wedding is a lot to organize when you're not feeling well. So is restructuring your life. If you want me to take on some of those tasks, I will. Fair warning, I'd likely opt for marrying in a courthouse as soon as I can arrange it. But I know your family is important to you. We'll talk again in a few days, when you've had time to get used to this news. But this is going to work, Rozi. You'll see."

She smiled, starting to believe him. Starting to recognize this gorgeous, expansive, promising emotion swelling within her. It was love. Hers was too shy and tentative to be acknowledged aloud. His feelings were even more deeply buried, but she wanted to believe that tender light in his eyes was the match to what was dawning within her.

Then she received news from her family that sent them plunging back to square one.

CHAPTER TEN

GISELLA FORWARDED THE press release and Rozi was reading about a truly horrific *admission of massive fraud* when Viktor appeared with his own tablet in hand.

His expression was so forbidding and cold, her heart clutched in her chest. Gone was the doting husband-to-be. This was the starkly aloof, dismissive man she had met that first night.

"I didn't know," she swore.

His jaw clenched and he only penetrated her skull with a furious stare.

"I don't even have anything to do with Benny's company," she said of her cousin. Benny was the eldest son of her boss, Uncle Ben, who owned the jewelry shop, and ground zero for this explosive news. "Benny is a geologist. Barsi Minerals is his baby. It's only associated to Barsi on Fifth in an arm's-length way, to allow some of our clients to invest in precious and rare metals."

"You don't get dividends?"

"Grandmamma bought all of us some shares when Benny was starting out. It was her way of supporting his venture. So yes, I get a few dividends, but it's not big money."

That wasn't entirely true. It was the only investment she had other than a very modest emergency fund in her savings account. She had always liked knowing she had those shares as a retirement nest egg. Now it was being smashed open and eaten by coyotes.

"Viktor, our reputation is very important to us. Gisella is saying that Benny is accepting responsibility, but his mistake was in trusting the wrong person. *He* didn't salt those mineral samples."

"And it's purely a coincidence that Kaine Michaels was set up to take the fall for this 'mistake.'"

"I don't know how he was pulled into it." Rozi had read between the lines on Gisella's email and suspected that Gizi was romantically involved with Kaine. Or had been, before Benny's crime tore them apart.

Kaine Michaels was washing his hands of all of them, leaving the Barsi family to face investigations and possible criminal charges. Benny was on the hook for massive fines and Gisella was worried that the shop wouldn't survive. All Rozi could think was that their grandmother would be devastated. Not just by the loss of her lifetime of work, but by what was happening to her grandson and the rest of them.

"I have interests in steel," Viktor said. "Was I to be the next mark?"

His accusation was a knife straight to the base of her throat. *"No."*

"We can't marry with this going on. I won't associate my family name with *that*." He threw his tablet onto an ottoman.

"Fine." She held his gaze, eyes so hot they ached, but she refused to blink.

"And I won't bail them out."

"Did I ask you to?"

"Now you know better than to try. I have to go to the office."

She barely saw him for days, not that she wanted to.

She felt horrid, sick all the time, exhausted, worried and homesick. She was miserable and couldn't go home because she would only be dragged into the scandal. Even her mother, who was so worried she couldn't speak without bursting into tears, was telling her to stay away until things settled down.

Rozi would have given anything to spill out all her worries to Viktor, but she was so afraid that he would think she was playing for his sympathy she could only isolate herself and suffer in silence. She went to bed early, avoided meals—which wasn't hard since everything turned her stomach—and watched TV in her room instead of joining him downstairs.

Finally, when she couldn't contain her anguish another minute, she called Gisella on the tablet, catching up to her properly for the first time since Gisella had gone to San Francisco and Rozi left for Hungary.

"How are the charges not cleared up yet?" Gizi asked her, sounding scandalized.

"That's just an excuse. I want to come home, Gizi. So much. But… Don't tell Mom, okay? I'm pregnant." It had been potentially exciting news—for a few days. Now it was exactly as distressing as she had feared it would become.

Gisella was stunned, of course. "What are you going to do?"

"Viktor said he wanted to marry me, but that was before…"

"Benny," Gisella provided.

"Yes. He won't make any announcements. It would impact his family and business. How bad is it there?"

"Bad. But we're figuring things out," Gisella assured her in the determined tone that was her signature. "It'll be messy and maybe we'll all move into your parents' house, but it'll bring us closer, right?"

It was a worst-case scenario and Rozi wanted to be there so bad, she nearly burst into tears.

"I miss everyone so much. I feel horrible, Gizi. Morning sick and so guilty I'm not there. I want to curl up and cry."

"Do you want me to come?"

"You can't, can you?" She swallowed, hopeful for about one minute before she realized it would likely only arouse Viktor's suspicions further.

"Probably not. The investigators might think I'm fleeing the country or something. We're being watched, Rozi. The investigators are probably monitoring this conversation right now. It's a total nightmare. You're smart to stay out of it as long as you can."

"I still feel horrible. And keeping this baby from Mom? She would want to come, but there's no way they can afford it." Especially if the modest income they all enjoyed from the shop had dried up. "I would far rather she paid Bea's tuition for Juilliard. There's nothing you or anyone can do here anyway."

"I could hold your hair," Gisella suggested with a quirky smile.

"Yeah, Viktor has about had it with that, I think." She couldn't bring herself to admit she barely saw him. His silent treatment was worse than everything else combined.

"Is he there right now?"

"No. He's at work."

"Rozi… Is it just morning sickness? Because you look…"

Like her heart was breaking? It was.

"Do you love him?" Gisella asked.

She did, she acknowledged with deep misery. She had fallen in love against her better judgment and she couldn't even tell him. He wouldn't believe her. He didn't trust her at all.

"It just happened, Gizi. I didn't mean to get pregnant. I know you and I promised each other—"

"Oh, my God, Rozi. I'm not judging. I was sleeping with Kaine. I know exactly how it happens. That was a silly promise we made as kids. No, I'm saying if you're not in love... This isn't Grandmamma's time. You can come home and we'll take care of you."

"How?" Rozi asked with an edge of hysteria. "Barsi on Fifth is going down the toilet. Viktor..." She sniffed. He had said he would set her up with a workshop when she was ready, but she doubted he'd help her now. She would have to look for work when she was feeling better. "For the sake of the baby—and Grandmamma—I should give marriage a try, shouldn't I? She married Grandpapa out of necessity. It can work."

"Are you trying to convince me or yourself?"

Herself.

"Look, there's actually more we need to talk about with the earrings," Gisella said.

"I know, but I think I'm going to be sick again," Rozi groaned as her stomach clenched and the clammy sweat of nausea descended over her. "I have to go. I'm sorry to dump all this on you and ask you to keep it secret. I had to talk it out. But it's better if everyone just thinks I'm stuck in limbo here. They have enough to worry about."

"I love you. I miss you."

"Me, too." She apologized again before she ended the call, then hurried to the bathroom to be sick. *Again.*

Viktor knew there was a damaged part of him that had been waiting for the other shoe to drop. He hadn't been surprised when her family scandal erupted. He hadn't even felt particularly betrayed. He had expected—maybe even *wanted*—something to happen that would prove Rozi was duplicitous after all. This way, his world view wouldn't be disturbed. He could stay comfortable in his cynicism. Superior, even. And secure from the emotional stabs of life.

But as with the first days of their acquaintance, Rozi defied his expectations. She didn't ask him for money to bail out her family, even though he watched her cousin's company implode like a nuclear bomb, leaving a giant crater in her family's livelihood. Their jewelry shop was forced to close its doors while their books were examined and the news coverage was extremely unkind.

Rozi didn't use the money he did give her, either. She didn't go shopping or try to use her connection to his name to salvage her family's position. She didn't ask him to take her out and show her a good time or see sites or look for a location for her own shop.

She left the house for doctor appointments and didn't even charge the cost of her iron supplements to his card. When he did see her, she looked miserable.

Because the one fact that remained true and undeniable was that she was pregnant with his child—and it was making her sick as hell.

They weren't sleeping together, so he couldn't help her in the night if she needed him. His one suggestion that she call him had been met with an appalled stare and an indignant "I can manage."

In the morning, if she showed up for breakfast, she was just as likely to turn green at some aroma and turn tail, not to be seen for an hour or more. He'd taken her back to the doctor, worried about her, and they'd said her nausea was not abnormal.

Not abnormal?

He'd pulled the doctor aside and torn a strip off him. He'd been given a bottle of electrolyte fluids and a phone number for house calls.

Dissatisfied with that answer, he made her an appointment with a specialist and came home early to collect her. He found her on the veranda, her tablet in her lap, her face buried in tissues as she cried her eyes out.

"What happened?"

She hadn't heard him coming. She leaped to her feet and her tablet flew to the concrete tiles, shattering the screen.

"Nooo!" She moaned, shoulders slouched. "Well, that's just great, isn't it?"

"I'll buy you a new one," he dismissed. It was nothing. Not worth that look of utter defeat on her face.

In fact, his concern for her health pushed him past worrying about entrapment and ploys.

"How much does your family need?" he asked flatly. "I'll set up the financing later today."

She had started to bend for the tablet, but straightened, expression stunned. Confused. "Why—? *No.*"

"What do you mean, no? The stress of your family situation is making your sickness worse."

"I don't want your money!" A spark of fiery spirit, the one he hadn't seen since she'd learned she was pregnant, flared briefly to life as she glared at him from red-rimmed eyes. "I don't want you to bail out my family or buy me a tablet. I don't want anything from you. *Nothing.*"

"Calm down." She was shaking. And her words sounded like a deeper rejection, threatening they were headed to a place they couldn't come back from. "What's going on? Who upset you? Who were you talking to?" He was glad the tablet was broken if it was upsetting her this badly.

She looked at the shards of glass with such hopelessness his heart clutched.

"Gisella is engaged to Kaine Michaels. *He* bailed out the shop."

Viktor reeled onto his heels, but before he could absorb this turn of events and know what to think of it, she choked out a harsh laugh.

"See, Gisella has secured us a mark. We no longer need *you*." The bitter sarcasm in her tone abraded like diamond grit. "My cousin has cold-bloodedly seduced a different billionaire into saving the family so we won't lose Grandmamma's lifetime of work. This pregnancy trap of mine was completely unnecessary."

"Stop it."

"It's what you're thinking!" she cried, wildly waving an arm. Her eyes grew brighter, lips trembling until she bit them. "Good thing you're so much smarter than him. Kaine Michaels is a fool, falling in l-love—"

She clapped a hand over her mouth and he tensed, hating when she was sick. *Hating* it.

But for once this wasn't a nausea spell. She was holding in emotion, an anguish that was so painful she closed her eyes and drew slow hissing breaths in her effort to withstand it.

Terror like he'd never known scythed through him, ghoulish and heart-stopping. "Is it the baby?"

He reached to take her arm, as if he could somehow keep her this side of a tragedy he didn't want to contemplate.

She jerked from his touch, like he was some kind of monster. "It's not that kind of pain," she choked.

She hugged herself and he realized with alarm how thin she was. Her jeans were loose, not hugged to her hips. Her wrists seemed even more delicate and her cheekbones jutted more prominently in her face. But of course she was losing weight. She barely ate and everything that went down came back up.

Fresh concern slammed through him. All he could think was that he had to get her to a doctor. Fix this. Make her well. Make her capable of smiling again.

"I came home to take you to the specialist," he reminded gruffly.

She might have whimpered, as though he was asking more of her than anyone should. Then she visibly tried to pull herself together, brushing her fingers under her eyes and drawing a congested breath.

"You're probably happy I'm being punished like this."

"For God's sake, how could you think that? Of course I'm not happy you're sick."

She didn't even look at him. Just stared at the broken tablet with such a dejected expression, he couldn't bear it.

"Come here." He held out his arms. His entire body hurt. He ached to hold her. Needed to. More than he needed his next breath.

She twitched her shoulder in rebuff, stepping back and turning away.

The action kicked his heart out of its hole. It sat askew in his chest, throbbing and raw.

"I haven't become any different just because Kaine bailed out my family," she said in a ragged voice. "Just because I don't need your money doesn't mean I'm not still the same opportunist you love to hate."

"I don't *hate* you." He ran his hand down his face, erasing the tension, but the constriction in his throat stayed there, turning his voice to gravel. "Stop upsetting yourself like this. You'll make yourself sick—"

But here it came, genuine nausea this time. She paled, groaned with frustrated agony and covered her mouth as she ran into the house.

He tipped back his head and drew a deep breath, trying to regain his equilibrium. Trying to put himself back together before she returned.

He didn't hate her. How could she think that?

You're probably happy I'm being punished like this.

Was that how she felt? *Punished?*

He was protecting himself, yes, but he hadn't seen his withdrawal as an action that could cause her pain.

When she didn't come back and they grew late for their appointment, he went searching for her. She was fast asleep, curled on her side on her bed, cheeks tracked with salt.

He draped a blanket over her, then sat on the edge of the bed, staring at her pale lips and the bruised circles under her eyes. He picked up a cool lock of her hair, not wanting to wake her, but needing to touch her, even if it was only a silky tress wound around his finger.

I haven't become any different just because Kaine bailed out my family.

How did he feel so outdone by a stranger's actions? Ashamed, even. Rozi had been worried about her family all this time. He had held off making offers, certain she would ask him for money, but she hadn't said a word. Had being right been so important to him?

He was programmed to protect the family assets. Her cousin's scandal had been a shock when it arose. He had reacted with exactly as much aggression and protectionism as he would if any other threat had arisen against Rika Corp.

But he shouldn't have turned his back on helping her even before she asked for it.

He hadn't meant this to become such a schism between them. He hadn't meant to put up such a wall between them that she thought he didn't care she was sick. That he was *glad* she was suffering. He couldn't bear how frail she seemed.

He leaned down to press the lightest of kisses against her cool, white cheek.

As he drew back, she came awake with a start, eyes flashing open. For one fraction of a second, a sleepy, welcoming light shone in her gaze. It was the warmth of sunrise, bathing him in a glow of promise. All the turmoil in him settled and he was renewed.

Then a deep vulnerability hollowed out her gaze. She broke eye contact, glancing around in confusion, rolling onto her back and sliding to put more distance between them.

"The appointment," she said in recollection. "I was only going to lie down for a minute while my stomach settled."

The shadows came back into his soul, like wraiths in their cold emptiness.

"Stay here. You obviously need the rest." He set his hand on her hip, trying to reassure her, but she was already rolling away, pushing off his touch with the tangle of the blanket, kicking her feet toward the far side of the mattress.

"I want to go. I read that it might be the vitamins. Maybe there's another kind I can take."

"Rozi," he said to her back, watching her stiffen at the gravity of his tone, but he needed to make one thing clear. "I know this pregnancy wasn't deliberate. I'm not happy you're sick. I want you to be well."

He waited, thinking maybe she would tell him how to make *them* well again, but when she spoke, she only said, "Then let's see what the doctor says."

The doctor prescribed antinausea pills that made her so drowsy, she started to nod off at the dinner table, completely missing whatever Viktor had been saying.

Viktor swore sharply, muttering, "This is impossible."
It was.

He helped her to bed, saying, "I'm going to call the doctor, see if we can try a lower dose."

Maybe it was the numbness of the pills. Maybe it was simply despair, but she heard herself say, "You said this would work. You're the one who can't be trusted."

She heard his breath suck in as though she'd stuck a knife in his belly, but maybe she imagined it. Her head hit the pillow and she fell into near unconsciousness.

But he was right that this was impossible, she decided over the next few days. They couldn't go on like this. *She* couldn't. Her heart had broken a little when she had read Gisella's email. Not because Kaine had acted where Viktor had initially refused. She didn't expect him to bail out strangers just because she happened to get herself pregnant with his child.

The fact that Kaine had been moved by his love for Gisella had filled her with happiness for her cousin, but anguish for herself. Gisella had what Rozalia wanted—a man who returned her love. Her cousin was marrying for love and when *they* made a baby, it would be an expression of their love for one another.

Not a chain that bound a pair of strangers into a lifetime of mistrust.

Part of Rozi still believed she should marry Viktor for their baby's sake, but her feelings ran deep enough that any tiny rebuff or dark look from him rent a hole inside her. His inability to trust her was already chipping away at her, making her future look so bleak she could hardly face it.

Maybe he no longer wanted marriage. They hadn't talked about it since Benny's scandal had broken, when Viktor had firmly rejected attaching his family name to her soiled one.

The more she dwelled on it, the more she knew she couldn't marry him. She might have to raise a baby with a man who didn't love her, but she couldn't live with him and sleep with him and stand by his side, suffering an eternity of silent anguish.

She almost took the coward's way out and left for New York without talking to him, but she knew it would only undermine his faith in her even more.

So she made her arrangements, packed, then had his car drop her outside Rika Corp's headquarters. She was shown directly into his empty office.

He joined her immediately, before she'd had a chance to take in more than an impression of mahogany relics and fine art that reflected his signature style of aristocracy and understated luxury.

"What's wrong?" he asked, clearly having been pulled from a meeting. He closed the door with a firm clip. "I thought your next appointment was a week from tomorrow." He reached inside his jacket for his phone while raking a sharp gaze from her face to her feet.

"That's not—" She linked her hands before her and tried to look calm and resolved when she was actually terrified and already beginning to miss him. "I'm going back to New York. For Gisella's engagement party."

His brows slammed together. "When?"

"The car is downstairs. I'm on my way to the airport."

"And you tell me this now?" He glanced toward the door he'd come through, looking as though his mind was trying to wrap up whatever he'd been discussing.

"I'm not asking you to come with me. In fact—"

He swung his attention back to her, his forbidding glare like a roundhouse kick to the face.

She licked her lips, clinging to her composure. "I'm not running away. I'm not. It's a return ticket. I plan to come back within a week. Unless you would prefer I stayed there."

"Of course it's not what I would prefer." His voice roughened and tightened with intensity. "If you had given me more than five minutes' notice, I would have arranged a charter and taken you myself. Give me an hour and I will."

"I don't want you to."

His head flung back as though she'd raked her nails down his cheek.

"I want you to stay here and believe me when I say I'm coming back." Her chest constricted as she threw down that gauntlet. Her grip was going to leave fingerprint bruises on the backs of her hands. "I want to prove to you that I can be trusted. It's the only way I can see us moving forward in—" her voice thinned and she fought to make it strong enough to be heard "—in any capacity."

He was not a slow man. His incisive brain was getting there before she had to spell it out.

"And what sort of capacity do you envision?" His expression was already altering with comprehension, hard and implacable, but she couldn't tell what he was thinking beneath that wall. Couldn't decipher what he was feeling. Not beyond umbrage and refusal to accept what she was saying before she'd even spoken the words.

She threw herself the final distance, into the very heart of the firestorm.

"I've found an apartment." Inside she writhed in agony. Only her voice revealed her pain, and only in its hollow emptiness. "I'm confident I can find a job to support myself. I don't expect you to pay my bills. We'll work out a custody arrangement before the baby is born."

He might have been gray beneath his normally swarthy tan, but her vision was fading in and out with anxiety.

"Now who is trying to punish?" he charged in a voice filled with gravel.

"That's not what this is." In fact, she was beseeching him for understanding. "We're barely speaking, Viktor. You're not even coming home for dinner."

"To eat alone?" His tone lashed sharp as a whip. He touched his forehead, then put his hand out in a halt, retaking hold of his own temper.

She looked to the floor, unable to deny that she was either too sick or fast asleep, so not much company.

"I know your concern for the baby is legitimate," she said, trying for calm. "You're worried about the pregnancy and want this baby as much as I do. I know that." Pressure gathered in her chest. "But I need to be wanted, too."

"You've been *sick*."

"I'm not talking about physically! I'm saying you don't want *me*. You wouldn't have leaped to all those suspicions so quickly, every time, if you had any regard for me. You don't want to believe in me," she accused. "You don't want to risk getting hurt, so you hold back, but you expect me to tie myself to a lifetime of being hurt by your accusations. I won't. I want to marry for love and you won't give me that."

He sucked in a breath as though her words had been a body blow. "Love is a lie. I refuse to lie to you. Be thankful *you* can trust *me*."

"Love is *real*," she cried, releasing the woman who knew when to abandon mediation and fight with the courage of her convictions. She pointed to the middle of her chest. "I've experienced it." So had he, if he would only open his heart to let it in. "But I'm starting to question whether I deserve to be loved." She shook her head, unwilling to descend into that pit of despair. "That's why I have to go home. I need to be with people who *do* love me. Just for a little while, before I can face you again."

He did go white then, visibly. But he didn't stop her when she walked out.

CHAPTER ELEVEN

AT SOME POINT, minutes or hours after Rozi had left, Viktor's PA rang through to ask if he would rejoin the conference call he had abruptly left.

His heart had leaped out of his throat at the news Rozi had tracked him down unexpectedly. He had known immediately that her reason for coming could only be bad news. That was all they had between them right now. Bad and worse.

He told his PA he would remain behind his locked door, then poured himself a drink and stared broodingly out the window. At some further point, the sky darkened so he was staring at a view of slate and black with pinpoints of light.

The day was gone and so was Rozi. He should have stopped her from leaving, but how?

I need to be with people who do *love me.*

He might not put stock in that emotion, but he believed she believed in it. And in that highly charged moment, he had seen they needed a breather. A reset of some kind. He'd been aware of that all week, since their last argument had ended on her pained, *You're the one who can't be trusted.*

Those words had been eating at him. Was this how she had been feeling since the mess with her family had come to light? Stung by a lack of faith so bitter all she could taste was gall? It was a terrible feeling.

The irony was, he hadn't been giving her the silent treatment as she seemed to think. He had been staying late to finalize a handful of projects and moving meetings so he could take a solid week off.

He had wanted to take her back to the mountains. She had seemed to like it there. Perhaps she would start sketching again. Why that was important to him, he had no idea, but he sensed that her work was intrinsic to her and that not doing it was akin to not eating or sleeping. Harmful at a basic level of survival.

Not that he was doing much beyond surviving himself. He *was* concerned about the baby. Constantly. But he was also worried about Rozi. He spent half the night listening for running water, the other half staring at the empty pillow beside him. What was he? A child? He didn't need a warm body to hold the monsters at bay.

But he wanted to hold her. Make love to her, certainly, but more than that, he couldn't relax without knowing whether she was sleeping peacefully or enduring more of that wretched nausea.

Now she would be half a world away. He hadn't had it in him to refuse her a visit with her family. In fact, he would have gladly taken her himself if she'd asked, but…

I want you to stay here and believe me when I say I'm coming back.

He knocked back his third? Fourth drink? Then set the glass on the edge of his desk and pushed his hands into his pockets.

If she had wanted to run away with his baby, she could have done it anytime before now. He had no doubts she would come back. He knew she would return as surely as he knew she would move into her own place when she did. And insist on paying all her bills herself. She was as impractical and idealistic as she claimed her parents to be. She would put herself into hardship to prove her point to him.

To deny him another avenue of suspicion or the opportunity to care for her the only way he could.

Did she understand that he didn't know *how* to give her what she needed?

This shouldn't be so hard! It sure as hell shouldn't be this painful.

I'm starting to question whether I deserve to be loved.

That hurt most of all. It hurt in a way he couldn't describe or endure. It was a psychic sort of pain, penetrating into the very depths of his being. Because even as he denied the existence of love, he believed that if anyone deserved to be loved, it was Rozi.

She was the embodiment of what he had once understood that emotion to be—generous and kind, empathetic and innately beautiful. Abstract and impossible to fully describe, yet stalwart and strong. Reliant. And joyously uplifting. She was capable of pressing laughter into his dry throat with a glance. And—he winced as something wrenched open inside his chest, forcing him to confront the gaping hole left by her absence—she was necessary to him.

He needed her.

Desperately.

You don't want to risk getting hurt, so you hold back, but you expect me to tie myself to a lifetime of being hurt.

And yet, what would he face without her? He was already in agony with a bedroom wall between them. Was he supposed to subsist on an impersonal weekly glimpse of her as they handed their child back and forth like a set of car keys? His first thought when he had realized she could be pregnant had been to lock her into his life so she could give his child what had been denied him. *Love.*

He hadn't consciously put that together, but he had

wanted her to express that emotion to his child and *teach him how to express it*.

Had he followed her examples? Not lately. No, he had only taught her how to question her own worth. He had driven her to seek love elsewhere because she had given up on his providing her a shred of it.

His damp gaze hit the ceiling and he released a feral cry of pain, straight from his tormented core. Janitors twelve flights below must have heard it. It left claws in his throat that made each following breath sting to the bottoms of his lungs.

Rozi hadn't heard it, though. Because he had let her go.

The front door of her parents' home was as wide-open as the arms that wrapped around her, strong and familiar. This was the succor she had yearned for. Within the hour, she had told her mother everything about Viktor Rohan except for the most intimate details of their brief history.

"You love him?" her mother asked, brows pulled into a slant of empathy.

"So much." Tears stung her eyes. "And I understand why he has a hard time trusting me, but I can't live my entire life under suspicion."

"Oh, darling." Her mother hugged her for the millionth time and rubbed her back. And even though her hug fixed nothing, it fixed everything.

Rozi's father came home and picked her up and spun her around, then did it again when she told him about the baby. She swore them to secrecy about her pregnancy. "I don't want to steal Gisella's thunder tonight. Let her and Kaine have their moment."

She had a nap and, a few hours later, joined all her family as they convened at Aunt Alisz's brownstone.

Predictably the extended family went crazy when they

saw her. Even more predictably, she burst into tears as she accepted one hug after another. She had missed them all so much!

"You're here alone?" Gisella asked as she squeezed her. "Is everything all right?"

"I'm going back in a week. I needed to see everyone, explain things to Mom. Don't say anything about anything, okay?" She drew her weepy self out of her cousin's embrace and introduced herself to Kaine. "Hi, I'm Rozi."

"I've heard a lot about you." She had seen photos, but it didn't prepare her for how wickedly handsome he was, especially when he smiled with genuine welcome and concern. "How are you?"

Apparently at least one other person knew she was pregnant. She shot Gizi a look. Gizi looked to the ceiling.

She had confided in Kaine because she trusted him. They were in love. It shone bright as a beacon from both of them.

Must be nice.

Rozi swallowed her envy and moved to sit with her grandmother. She had no intention of bringing up the earrings, but her grandmother said, "You two girls have been up to things. You should have told me."

Grandmamma could have been talking about Rozi's arrest or the search for the earrings or the true story behind them. Rozi pressed one frail hand gently between her two warmer ones.

"We love you. I hope you know that. But yes, we've been up to things. Can I come by tomorrow to explain?"

"There's no rush. You only just got back."

Rozi appreciated her grandmother's reluctance to delve into painful memories, but she would soon reveal that she was only home to quit her job and sublet her apartment, and *why*. Grandmamma would need to hear that firsthand

and soon because she would need as much notice as possible to get used to the idea.

"Oh, my word!" her grandmother gasped, trembling fingers pulling away to touch her collar.

"What—?" Rozi looked over her shoulder and gasped, as well. "It's not a ghost!" she hurried to reassure her grandmother. Although her own heart leaped as though the grim reaper himself had shown up for her soul. "It's Viktor."

"The man who put you in jail?"

"And got me out," she clarified, heart soaring and sinking, swooping every direction as she drank in the way Viktor took command of the room simply by entering it. His tailored suit clung to his powerful frame and if his eyes looked deeply set and bruised from travel, it only added to his air of dangerous mystique.

She didn't ask herself what he was doing here, though. It was devastatingly obvious why he was here.

He didn't trust her.

Viktor knew his mistake the second his searching gaze found the somber pair of eyes he was looking for. Beneath her surprise lurked accusation and worse, disappointment.

Believe me when I say I'm coming back.

The ache in his chest intensified. This wasn't a failure to trust. He had had one thought from the second he had realized he loved Rozalia. *Get to her.*

The young woman who looked like Rozi and had let him in the door stopped in front of her. She planted her hands on her hips. "This is Viktor Rohan. He's looking for his *fiancée*. Does Mom know?"

Rozi gave her an exasperated look. "I said I would tell you everything later, Bea! This is Gisella's day." Rozi stood and gave him a faltering smile. "You've met my sister."

She let her hair fall forward to hide her expression as she bent to help an elderly woman rise from the sofa. "Grandmamma, this is Istvan's great-nephew, Viktor Rohan. My grandmother, Eszti Barsi."

Her grandmother set her cool, frail hand on his cheek.

"So much like him." She smiled mistily, her eyes filled with a glow that seemed vaguely familiar to Viktor. Rozi had her eyes, he realized.

She loved Istvan very much, he could hear Rozi saying.

The light he saw in this aged pair of eyes was poignant and faded by time, not directed at him, but by the memory he inspired in her. He had caught glimpses of something like this incandescence in Rozi's eyes, though. A potent and fierce version that had been achingly beautiful and painfully absent since her family's troubles had torn them apart.

Since he had rejected her for no crime except his own presumption she would commit one.

"You're marrying our Rozi?" Eszti looked to her granddaughter. "You girls have been up to *many* things."

"It's a long story, Grandmamma. We'll come by tomorrow for a proper visit and I'll tell you everything," Rozi promised. "But I should introduce Viktor to Mom and Dad."

She took him into the kitchen to meet her mother, then to the barbecue, where her father was mastering the grill. Both were surprised and welcoming. Rozi had obviously told them about the baby.

She drew him away to a corner of the garden as soon as she could.

"Those are usually comfort smells for me, but not today." She set her fist against her tight lips.

"Did you take a pill?"

"I let it wear off so I wouldn't be in a coma for this party."

"Do you want to leave?"

"No." She blinked eyes damp with frustration and hurt.

"I'm not here to take you away," he said through his teeth. "It was time I met your family." He searched her gaze, uncertain how to salvage their relationship. He had thought coming here would prove he cared enough to follow her, but—

"Rozi," a woman called from above them on the veranda. She was willowy with caramel-colored hair and held the hand of a man Viktor recognized as Kaine Michaels. Gisella tucked her hair behind her ear, head cocked in silent question. "Come tell me about the earring."

"You've come all this way," Rozi said, offering Viktor an ironic smile. "You might as well meet your cousins."

They made the rounds, and while Viktor earned sharp looks of curiosity, everyone was their warm, loving self toward both of them. Even so, Rozi found it excruciating.

Viktor might have a point that it was time he met her parents, but his coming here was still a giant billboard advertising his complete lack of faith in her.

As such, Rozi couldn't relax. He was attentive, hovering protectively, but that only made her wonder if it was a show for her family. Then she hated herself for doubting his sincerity. He worried about her. Physically. Or at least, he worried about the baby.

She gripped her elbows defensively as she introduced him to Aunt Alisz, then left them chatting about his mother as she excused herself to the powder room where she tried to pull herself together.

When she came back, Viktor was in discussion with Gisella. It didn't surprise her. Men were always drawn to her more sophisticated cousin, but it stung worse than usual.

"How did you make out with the earring?" Kaine asked, intercepting her.

"Hmm?" She dragged her gaze off the pair. "Oh, like I said to Gizi, I don't think here is the place to compare notes. I don't want to upset Grandmamma."

Kaine's mouth twitched. He tugged his earlobe again. "I'm using your code. I want a private conversation. To ask you something."

"Oh." She blinked, then chuckled. "You must be very special if Gizi has shared *that* with you." It was a signal they'd developed in childhood and still used occasionally if they happened to be stuck in a conversation and wanted rescue. "Careful, though. If she catches you, she's liable to think you're asking her to get *you* out of talking to *me*."

"Let's be quick then, before she comes over." He told her what he wanted and she answered quickly as Viktor and Gisella came across to join them.

"We've been invited for brunch tomorrow," Gisella said, taking Kaine's arm. "At your hotel," she informed Rozi with a perplexed smile. "I thought I was coming to your apartment in the morning, to help you start closing it up."

Rozi sent Viktor a look that silently said, *See?* She had every intention of tying off loose threads here and going back to Budapest.

"Sounds great," Kaine said smoothly into the stilted silence.

As for Viktor's presumption that she would stay with him at his hotel, she didn't bother arguing that. No sense in ruining a perfectly good party.

But they would have to talk this out sooner than later. She was already suffering a pit of dread in her gut and wanted it over with.

"We should say good night." Rozi smiled wanly at Viktor. "Quit while I'm ahead."

His gaze sharpened as though he knew she was feeling well enough to stay and was cutting short their evening for other reasons.

"If you're sure." He took his time as he drew out his phone. "I'll call for my car."

Gisella hugged her and Rozi told her mother she was leaving. Moments later, they slipped away.

Her bag was at her mother's, but after their talk she could take a cab back there, so Rozi sat quietly beside him, not speaking until they walked into his penthouse at the five-star hotel.

The suite held plush furniture in a large sitting room, crown moldings and brass fixtures and cherrywood side tables topped with fresh flowers. There was a dining area and two bedrooms, each with a massive bed and a gorgeous en suite bathroom full of marble and thick white towels on heated rods.

When she came back to the lounge from exploring, she joined him overlooking the view of snaking lights glowing between the tufts of Central Park's darkened treetops.

"What did you think of Aunt Alisz and Gisella?" she asked curiously.

"We don't need a blood test. Alisz is exactly like my mother."

Despite his flat assessment, she smiled. "That's what I thought when I met your mother. I found her strangely endearing for it."

"What were you and Kaine talking about?"

Whatever lightness had briefly elevated her spirits drained away. "Really?"

The disdain in her tone had him snapping his head to look down at her.

"For one solitary minute, I let myself think…" She walked away, chest tight. She went all the way to the other side of the suddenly too-small living area, then flung around to confront him. "Are you genuinely suspicious of me having a conversation with a man at his own engagement party? One who's marrying a woman who consistently outdoes me when it comes to male attention? You came a long way to deliver another insult, Viktor. *I* should be asking *you* what you were talking to Gisella about, since you went straight to her the second my back was turned."

"I would never hurt you like that." He threw his head back with insult. "I will *never* step out on you. Ever."

Distantly, she knew that was probably true, given the betrayal he'd suffered at the hands of his first love and his brother, but all she could say was a tormented, "Why the hell would I give you the chance to? You can't even—"

"I trust you!" he cut in, pinching the bridge of his nose. "I came all this way to tell you that. To make you believe it."

"And started by asking why I was talking to another man? Kaine wanted me to make Gisella's rings. Okay? That's what we were talking about. He wanted to surprise Gisella and that's why we quit talking when you two came up." She looked blindly toward the blackened windows.

After a pulse of silence, he said, "That's what I asked Gisella to do."

"You asked her to make rings for me?" She had to drag her brain back from wondering where she would sleep tonight and looked blankly at him. "Why?"

"Because you're too sick to do it yourself. What did you tell Kaine?"

"That I'm too sick. And that I don't have a workshop. And that Gizi probably wants to design them herself, especially if he plans to wear one, so she can match them."

"Is that what you would prefer?"

"Viktor…" Hopelessness overwhelmed her.

"I can't buy your rings from a shop, can I? You'll only return them." He ran his hand through his hair, seeming flummoxed. Maybe even edging toward despair.

"But I told you," she began with a tremor in her chest.

"Don't say you won't marry me." He closed his eyes and his voice was so hushed, it was a prayer. His hand fisted as though he was enduring great pain. "Don't tell me you're not coming back."

CHAPTER TWELVE

"YOU WOULDN'T LET me stay. Would you?" Her natural optimism flared, sensing a turning point. She waited for him to say of course he wouldn't let her stay. He loved her and couldn't bear to let her go.

But as silence greeted her question, she knew herself to be deluded. Her last spark of hope was gutted in an agonizing burn, leaving her abandoned in a wasteland of loneliness.

"I don't know what to do anymore." Viktor braced his hands on the back of the sofa, arms wide, head hanging, shoulders looking ready to buckle under a weight. "I haven't seen you smile in weeks. Then, tonight... You were radiant." The beds of his fingernails were white where he dug them into the sofa. "I wasn't *suspicious* when you were talking to Kaine. I was jealous for an entirely different reason."

A despairing noise choked in her throat.

He picked up his head and shook it in a way that seemed like indulgent affection. Gentle exasperation, maybe.

"Men look at you, Rozi. Never doubt your attraction. Everyone notices you. You don't see it, which is part of your charm, but *everyone* wants to be near you. I didn't think you were flirting with your cousin's fiancé," he dismissed. "I was jealous because you were smiling at him. I can't remember when you last smiled at me. Maybe I deserve that. I know I've hurt you. But that's why I asked what you were talking about. I wanted to know what made you smile. I wanted some crumb of your life that isn't the suffering I've inflicted on you."

"Oh, Viktor." She sank into the armchair, defeated. "This isn't something you've done to me." She was the idiot who had fallen in love with a man who had warned her he had no heart.

"Like hell it isn't! Every day I think I'll be lucky if you survive this pregnancy. I thought the morning sickness was what had sucked away that brightness in you. Or your family's troubles. I thought that once the baby came, you'd come back to life. But that's not what's eating away at you. It's *me*."

She couldn't deny it. Could only swallow back her unrequited love, drained and grief-stricken by the effort.

"I'm killing you by inches. I saw that tonight and it tears me up. I can't make you come home with me, but I can't imagine going home without you." He clenched his jaw, looking as though he was taking a whipping and refusing to let his cries break free from his locked throat.

"Because of the baby?" She could hardly breathe. "I promised you I would go back. I'll keep my word. You'll see your child, Viktor. Every day if—"

"I want *you*." He looked like he would snap the sofa in two. "In my bed. In my life. *Every day*. But I don't know how to keep you without destroying you."

Nothing crushed her like pain. Especially when the people she loved suffered. In that way, she was exactly like those who had made her. She couldn't witness his agony and not want to alleviate it.

"Oh, Viktor." She buried her face in her hands but knew she would have to release her heart to him. Lay it bear and accept the imperfection and inequality of their feelings for one another.

"Don't cry. Please don't cry." She looked up to see him taking the seat opposite her.

"I'm not crying. But, Viktor, I—"

"Wait. Shh. Let me do something. Will you give me your hands?" He held out his own.

She tentatively set her trembling fingers on his open palms. Swallowed the thickness in her throat.

"I know you have every reason to hate me—"

"I don't hate you. I lo—"

"Shh. Let me say this. I shouldn't have made presumptions that day when you found out about your family's trouble. I'm ashamed that I took so long to act. You were worried and I should have taken that burden from you. It was wrong and I won't let anything like that happen again, no matter where in the world you live."

"I'll live with you." She bit her lips to keep them from quivering. "If that's what you want, I will come home with you."

"Because you want to believe in me. That's who you are. But you're afraid. Because I've damaged your trust in me. But listen." He took a shaky breath. Dropped his mask so she could see the deep chasm of lonely agony inside him. It was so vast, her own heart pulsed with pain. She instinctively clung to his hands, unwilling to let him fall into that cavern.

He looked down at her touch, smiling faintly. "I'm going to say it first, to prove I really do trust you." He closed his hands over hers, so they were clinging tightly to each other. He looked into her eyes. "I love you, Rozi. I love you and I want you to love me back. I think you did, for a short while, but I fear I've killed it. I keep thinking if I can only keep you with me long enough, I *hope*—"

She launched herself into him.

"Ah, Rozi!" He gathered her in and they held one another in crushing arms, her damp cheek against his rougher one. It was pain and relief, a wrench as the final shields fell away between them, but healing as they pressed into one another.

"Loving hurts," she told him, wincing and shifting so her breasts weren't totally mashed.

"It does." He settled her sideways on his lap, touching one chaste kiss to her mouth before tilting his forehead against her brow. "You humble me."

"That's not what I want to do."

"I know. That's why you do." The reverent luminosity in his eyes was so bright, it brought tears to her own. "I'm in awe of you. Of your bravery and astonishing capacity to love. I need your love, Rozi. I need you in my life. It's terrifying to me how badly I need you. That's why I fought it."

"I know. But I do love you. I *miss* you."

"I'm right here. And I won't lock you out again. Does it help to know, though, that pushing you away taught me how badly I need you?"

"I thought I was just an awful person to be around." She poked out her tongue at how unpleasant her nausea made her feel.

"You're not awful." He frowned a scold. "You're sick. And if one more doctor tells me you're fine, I'm going to break every bone in his body."

"I'm fine right now," she said with a suggestive lean into him and a sweep of flirty lashes.

"Are you?" He kissed the corner of her damp eye. "Because it's enough to hold you again. We don't have to—"

She whispered in his ear.

He stood up with her in his arms. "I can definitely accommodate that."

She chuckled and kissed his throat as he carried her to the nearest bed.

When he set her upon it, he did so with veneration. Tenderness and gratitude and love enveloped her as they kissed and caressed, slowly undressing each other. They moved without hurry, impassioned, but letting each moment stretch out. Giving each strand of trust time to anchor and bind and thicken between them. With each kiss and caress, belief in each other seeped into the marrow of their bones.

When they were naked and united, she cupped the sides of his head in her hands. The unguarded emotion in his gaze transfixed her.

"I wasn't looking for an earring," she realized with awe. "I was searching for my soul mate."

"You found him. He's never letting you go again."

They began to move, celebrating the force that had pulled the two of them into a single space and made them, finally and for all time, one.

"It's a big ask," Rozi said to Gisella the next day.

She sidled a glance to Viktor that invited him to laugh with her at the way she had taken her cousin aback. That playful smile did things inside his chest, creaking open doors that let bursts of sunshine crash in. He didn't know how to be this happy. It made him feel foolish, but he wouldn't give up this expansive, bright view of the world for anything.

"Of course I want to." Gisella blinked her long lashes, visibly moved. "I always presumed I would be your maid of honor." She hugged her. "And this is perfect timing, since everyone is in town for a few more days. That hardly ever happens anymore."

"Not a double wedding with us?" Kaine suggested with a teasing look toward Gisella's.

"A kind offer, but we don't want to wait," Viktor said. He had Rozi's hand in his and caressed her knuckles with his thumb. His urgency wasn't driven by uncertainty. They'd been naked in the dark, reconnecting emotionally after their physical intimacy. He had asked her to marry him.

I want to marry you, Rozi. The fact we're expecting is pure icing.

What if we married before we go back, since everyone is in town?

He had carefully crushed her soft body into his own, whispering, *I'd marry you this minute if I could.*

"If we wait to plan something bigger, *I'll* be bigger," Rozi pointed out, wrinkling or nose. "Or I'd be trying to nurse in a wedding gown."

"You don't mind staying an extra few days?" Gizi asked of Kaine.

"Staying is the easy part," Kaine said. "Planning a wedding in a day and a half sounds like the challenge."

"Piece of cake," Gisella said with a confident wave.

Rozi stood and Viktor rose with her, immediately on alert.

"I'm fine," she hurried to assure him. "I just want my phone."

"When she's sick, she's really sick," Viktor said to Gisella, staying on his feet until Rozi came back.

"And when I take a pill, I need a four-hour nap. Then I'm fine for a while. Like now." She smiled at him, in good spirits despite the fact she'd been sick in the early hours this morning.

He had somehow gotten a pill into her before they had gone back to bed. She had slept late but had risen to shower and eat brunch with genuine appetite. Now she positively glowed.

"I always thought we'd have babies at the same time, but you're scaring me." Gisella eyed her. "Sorry, lover. I may never try it," she added to Kaine, but said it with a cheeky grin and a quick kiss to let him know she was joking.

"Your mom wasn't sick. You'll probably be fine," Rozi dismissed.

"Is your mother coming?" Gisella asked Viktor. "After meeting you, my mother is curious about her."

"I spoke to her this morning. She's bringing my aunt. They're catching a flight in a few hours."

"Oh, Grandmamma will like that." Gisella nodded approval. "Your story is so amazing, don't you think? Eszti's granddaughter is marrying Istvan's great-nephew. It's almost as if a higher power had a hand in bringing you two together."

"Viktor doesn't believe in fate," Rozi said, reaching for his hand to squeeze, silently telling him she was okay with his skeptical side, but she had changed him.

"I *didn't* believe in fate," he corrected, lifting her hand to his lips, adding truthfully, "I do now."

EPILOGUE

"MAMA?" ESTER QUESTIONED Viktor as he drew her out of her car seat a block from Barsi in Budapest.

"You know exactly where we are, don't you? Little smarty-pants." His heart swelled with love. Pride, too. Their daughter was only just learning to talk, but her curious gaze was always taking in the world, pointing and exploring and yes, sometimes getting into things she shouldn't. His wallet was a favorite along with her mother's purse. But her tiny arms were quick to deliver an exuberant squeeze of his neck and something as simple as her excitement at visiting her mother at the shop made a chuckle rattle in his chest.

He felt the same adoration and admiration for his wife. Her shop was an enormous success. The location and business plan had been carefully finalized after her morning sickness had let up in her second trimester. The doors had been opened days before she went into labor and she had recently hired more staff, including two new designers. Rozi worked part-time around their daughter's needs and any of his work commitments that required her presence at his side. She managed a few custom pieces a month, most of them on commission since she was in high demand.

"Our favorite browser is here." The saleswomen offered smiles of greeting when they entered, even though it was minutes before the shop was due to close for the day and Ester's presence guaranteed them an hour of polishing fingerprints off glass and shiny trim.

Viktor set Ester on her feet and she toddled quickly to the door of steel bars that guarded the back of shop. She grasped two and stuck her face between them.

"Mama!"

Rozi's rich laugh sounded, accompanied by a man's surprised one.

"I'm coming, sweet pea," Rozi called. She appeared moments later behind the bars.

The man with her seemed about Rozi's age. He was tall and well dressed and abruptly hugged Rozi, delivering a heartfelt "Thank you."

"Oh." Rozi stiffened in surprise, then patted his back. "Of course. It's my job."

They came through the door, Rozi flashing Viktor a glance that invited him to laugh at the stranger's effusive goodbye before she picked up Ester and gave her a much more enthusiastic hug of greeting. "How was daddy-daughter day?"

"Excellent." Viktor had wanted to be a more involved parent than his own, and while he thrived in being a unit with Rozi, he always enjoyed his one-on-one time with Ester.

"What do I owe you?" the young man asked.

"Nothing," Rozi said, brushing off the offer. "If you want a formal appraisal, you can book an appointment." She gave him the price. "That was just my educated opinion. Good luck."

"Thank you," he said with deep sincerity and what might have been relief. After a self-conscious nod at Viktor, he departed.

"He bought an engagement ring from a widower," Rozi

said as the door chimed shut. "His neighbor who needed the money. Then he worried it was fake or he had paid too much."

"And you set his mind at ease. As you do." He wrapped his arm around her waist as she came close enough to kiss him in greeting, still carrying Ester.

You don't owe me explanations, he conveyed with a brief moment of eye contact. People loved his wife. Family, friends, strangers, it didn't matter. They all took to her and trusted her and he couldn't resent or feel threatened when he was the most smitten of all.

"Look?" Ester asked, pointing.

"Yes, you can look. *Just* look. No touch," Rozi warned, setting Ester on her feet.

"That'll work. It always does," Viktor said, settling his arm around her again.

"I know, right?"

Ester could barely see into the cases, but that hadn't stopped her from poking a hand into an open drawer one day when Rozi had been with a customer. Rozi had caught her in time to pull a tennis bracelet out of her mouth.

Rozi relaxed into him, exhaling with contentment as they watched Ester plaster her little hands and button nose against a glass case.

"That was me, when I was her age. Oh!" Rozi recollected. "Gizi called. I said we were thinking of coming to see the baby. She's checking with Kaine for dates."

"Let me know. I'll make myself available. You haven't seen family in a while. I know you miss them."

"Excuse me," she admonished lightly, shifting so both her arms were around his waist and she was pressed to his front. "I'm with my family every day." She kissed his chin.

He closed his arms around her, trying not to let their sexual charge affect him too deeply here in front of their daughter and her employees. He couldn't entirely hide how deeply she moved him, though. He stroked her hair back from her face, tenderness and love suffusing him.

"And I am grateful for that every day. For you." He kissed her lightly.

"Me, too, for you." She smiled up at him with the radiant happiness that warmed him to the center of his being. "Shall we go home?"

It *was* a home, thanks to her.

"If we can pry your daughter out of here without a scene, yes."

"I think we both know that is an unreasonable expectation."

"Also your genes, I presume?"

"So much," she agreed sheepishly.

"I look forward to wearing her designs in ten or twelve years' time."

Ester made her first painted macaroni necklace two years later. Her father proudly wore it to his office the next day.

* * * * *

MILLS & BOON

Coming next month

A CINDERELLA TO SECURE HIS HEIR
Michelle Smart

'Do not misunderstand me. Getting custody of Domenico is my primary motivation. He is a Palvetti and he deserves to take his place with us, his family. In my care he can have everything but if custody were all I wanted, he would already be with me.'

She took another sip of her drink. Normally she hated whisky in any of its forms but right then the burn it made in her throat was welcome. It was the fire she needed to cut through her despair. 'Then what *do* you want? I think of all the work we've done, all the hours spent, all the money spent–'

'I wanted to get to know you.'

She finally allowed herself to look at him. '*Why*?'

The emerald eyes that had turned her veins to treacle lasered into hers. He leaned forward and spoke quietly. 'I wanted to learn about you through more than the reports and photographs my investigators provided me with.'

'You had me investigated?'

'I thought it prudent to look into the character of the person caring for my nephew.'

Her head span so violently she felt dizzy with the motion.

He'd been spying on her.

She should have known Alessio's silence since she'd refused his offer of money in exchange for Dom had been ominous. She'd lulled herself into a false sense of security and underestimated him and underestimated the lengths he would be prepared to go to.

Everything Domenico had said about his brother was true, and more.

Through the ringing in her ears, he continued. 'Do not worry. Any childhood indiscretions are your own concern. I only wanted to know about the last five years of your life and what I learned about you intrigued me. It was clear to me from the investigators' reports and your refusal of my financial offer that you had an affection for my nephew...'

'Affection does not cover a fraction of the love I feel for him,' she told him fiercely.

'I am beginning to understand that for myself.'

'Good, because I will never let him go without a fight.'

'I understand that too but you must know that if it came to a fight, you would never win. I could have gone through the British courts and made my case for custody—I think we are both aware that my wealth and power would have outmatched your efforts—but Domenico is familiar with you and it is better for him if you remain in his life than be cut off.'

She held his gaze and lifted her chin. 'I'm all he knows.'

He raised a nonchalant shoulder. 'But he is very young. If it comes to it, he will adapt without you quickly. For the avoidance of doubt, I do not want that outcome.'

'What outcome *do* you want?'

'Marriage.'

Drum beats joined the chorus of sound in her head. 'What on *earth* are you talking about?'

He rose from his seat and headed back to the bar. 'Once I have Domenico in Milan it will be a simple matter for me to take legal guardianship of him.' He poured himself another large measure and swirled it in his glass. 'I recognise your genuine affection for each other and have no wish to separate you. In all our best interests, I am prepared to marry you.'

Dumbfounded, Beth shook her head, desperately trying to rid herself of all the noise in her ears so she could think properly. 'I wouldn't marry you if you paid me.'

Continue reading
A CINDERELLA TO SECURE HIS HEIR
Michelle Smart

Available next month
www.millsandboon.co.uk

COMING SOON!

We really hope you enjoyed reading this book. If you're looking for more romance, be sure to head to the shops when new books are available on

Thursday 2nd May

To see which titles are coming soon, please visit

millsandboon.co.uk/nextmonth

MILLS & BOON

LET'S TALK
Romance

For exclusive extracts, competitions
and special offers, find us online: